A noise like a screen door smacking the wall sounded from behind the home...

"Grab the shotgun out of my truck," Rory said. It was taking a risk going after whoever had bolted out the back door. He didn't like leaving Emerson alone, not even with her aunt, in case there was someone else inside the home. "Be careful."

He ran around the side in time to hear dogs barking as someone flew past. Visibility wasn't a problem with all the chain-link fencing. He caught a glimpse of someone as he—based on his physical build and size—disappeared between a pair of houses several homes down the block. It would be too easy for him to circle back if Rory gave chase. And this person was fast, basically a blur. The thought of leaving Emerson alone and vulnerable despite her ability to shoot didn't sit well.

A scream of terror got Rory moving quickly back the way he came...

All my love to Brandon, Jacob and Tori, who are the great loves of my life. To Samantha, for the bright shining light that you are. You are also brave and I love having you as part of this family!

To Babe, my hero, for being my best friend, my greatest love and my place to call home. I love you with everything that I am. Always and forever.

Finally, to Katya and Arkadiy. Yours is one of my favorite love stories and I am blessed beyond measure to call you my friends.

RIDING SHOTGUN

USA TODAY Bestselling Author
BARB HAN

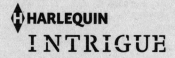

HARLEQUIN
INTRIGUE

♦ HARLEQUIN®
INTRIGUE™

Recycling programs
for this product may
not exist in your area.

ISBN-13: 978-1-335-58258-4

Riding Shotgun

Copyright © 2023 by Barb Han

For questions and comments about the quality of this book,
please contact us at CustomerService@Harlequin.com.

Harlequin Enterprises ULC
22 Adelaide St. West, 41st Floor
Toronto, Ontario M5H 4E3, Canada
www.Harlequin.com

Printed in U.S.A.

USA TODAY bestselling author **Barb Han** lives in north Texas with her very own hero-worthy husband, three beautiful children, a spunky golden retriever/standard poodle mix and too many books in her to-read pile. In her downtime, she plays video games and spends much of her time on or around a basketball court. She loves interacting with readers and is grateful for their support. You can reach her at barbhan.com.

Books by Barb Han

Harlequin Intrigue

The Cowboys of Cider Creek

Rescued by the Rancher
Riding Shotgun

A Ree and Quint Novel

Undercover Couple
Newlywed Assignment
Eyewitness Man and Wife
Mission Honeymoon

An O'Connor Family Mystery

Texas Kidnapping
Texas Target
Texas Law
Texas Baby Conspiracy
Texas Stalker
Texas Abduction

Visit the Author Profile page at Harlequin.com.

CAST OF CHARACTERS

Emerson Bennett—The search for her mother puts a target on her back.

Rory Hayes—He is committed to helping Emerson dig up the past, but how will he introduce his twelve-year-old daughter to his family when they didn't know she ever existed?

Liv Hayes—This twelve-year-old is about to meet the family she never knew.

Deputy Theo—Is he good at keeping secrets or actually in on the crime?

Bynum Ross—The owner of the bait and tackle store is hiding something.

Jimmy Zenon—This childhood friend of Rory's might be involved in a cover-up.

Chapter One

One photograph had turned the life Emerson Bennett had known for nearly thirty years on its head, shifting her world into chaos. A woman holding an infant, beaming. The baby in the picture was Emerson and she had no idea about the woman except the knowledge she was Emerson's mother. Strange, because she'd grown up with the belief her mother had died in a car crash, and the photos in frames around the house had a very different woman in them.

A need for answers brought her to the small Texas town of Cider Creek and to an even smaller convenience store, B-T, which she assumed stood for Bait and Tackle since that was the main advertisement. There was a two-handle gasoline pump out front, and the store window promised ice, snacks and soft drinks.

The smell of worms and dirt struck her the moment she opened the glass door. A bell jingled but the large-framed attendant who looked old enough to be her father barely glanced in her direction.

"Excuse me." Emerson stepped toward the gentle-man in overalls who stood behind the counter. The man was tall, six feet two inches if she had to guess. Sunspots dotted the skin of his face. Timeworn skin hung on a sturdy frame. He had the body of a man who knew a hard day's work.

He mumbled something unintelligible as he flipped the page of the fishing magazine he was browsing. She had a name and this address. The links to the woman in the picture weren't so clear.

Emerson approached the counter, her gaze steady on the man.

"Are you Bynum Ross, by chance?" she asked.

Without making eye contact, the man reached for an object on the opposite side of the cash register. He produced a small key attached to a big orange plastic bauble with Ladies written on it in black per-manent marker.

"Mr. Ross, I'm not here to use the restroom," she said, a little more insistent this time.

The man dropped his hand to the counter with a clunk as the key hit the glass. He held up a finger, halting her next words in favor of continuing his reading. A couple of beats later, he lifted his gaze. For a split second, she could have sworn recognition dawned, which made no sense because Emerson was certain she had never seen this man before. She'd never been to Cider Creek, and as far as she knew, never met any of the town's residents.

"Do you know me?" she asked, tilting her head to one side.

"No," he said quickly, a little too quickly.

She didn't respond, contemplating if he'd just lied.

"What can I help you with, *darlin'*?" he asked, regaining his composure in a heartbeat.

She bit back the urge to tell him the first thing he could do for her was not call her *darlin'*. Being addressed like a four-year-old at nearly thirty was like fingernails on a chalkboard. Getting answers trumped pride, so she cleared her throat and started over.

"Since you didn't correct me before, I'm hoping that means you are Bynum Ross." As she spoke, his grip around the orange plastic bathroom key bauble caused his knuckles to turn white.

Mr. Ross gave an almost imperceptible nod, but his lips and eyes told the real story. His gaze narrowed and his lips compressed into a frown. Obviously, he wasn't happy to see her.

"I'm looking for someone," she started. She'd rehearsed half a dozen lines on her way here from Arlington, where she'd grown up with a single father. Now saying the words out loud caused her tongue to stick to the roof of her mouth.

"Looks like you found him," he said, crossing his arms over his chest as he studied her. All hope he would be cooperative flew out the window given the chilly reception she received so far.

The bell on the door jingled as Emerson's pulse

kicked up a couple of notches. All she had to do was remember to breathe and she could do this. The hope of figuring out who the woman was in the photo she'd found tucked behind another in a frame as she'd gone through her dad's things spurred a boost of confidence.

"Not exactly. It's not you," she said before pulling the photo out of her purse and setting it on top of the counter. "I'm trying to locate the woman in the picture, and I thought you might know who she is."

Mr. Ross balked. He barely glanced at the photo before shoving it toward her as though it might bite.

"No idea what you're talking about," he said briskly. "Now, if you'll excuse me, I have to get back to work."

Emerson looked around. There was one customer inside the shop and none at either of the pumps. The physical presence of the man at the wall of coolers behind her filled the room. She didn't dare turn to get a good look at the distraction. Instead, she quirked a brow as she turned to face Mr. Ross.

"Is there anyone in town you could recommend that I speak to?" she asked. "It's important that I find this woman. It's personal."

"Not one," he said as he shrugged her off like she was an irritating fly on a horse's backside.

"Sir, please. Any information you have that might help me in my search would be much appreciated." She wasn't above begging after, while at her father's wake, she'd overheard her aunt say what a shame it was that Emerson had no idea who her real mother was. Grieving, Emerson could have sworn she'd heard wrong. After subtly confronting her aunt, who denied she'd said anything of the sort, Emerson's suspicions grew. Her aunt's dishonesty was a huge red signal.

And then Emerson had found the picture that was so old it was literally stuck to the one in front of it. She'd peeled the second layer off to find a woman holding and beaming at infant Emerson while standing in front of B-T.

So, she was here for answers. She had no idea how she was going to get them out of the stubborn man behind the counter. But returning to Arlington empty-handed after coming this far couldn't be the way this day ended. There were too many questions buzzing around inside her head, penetrating her thoughts, disturbing her sleep. She couldn't walk away from her only lead. Every person had a right to know the basics about themselves: their name, where they're from, who their real parents are. If what her aunt had spoken in hushed tones that cold November afternoon was true, Emerson had been lied to her entire life by the one person she'd trusted implicitly. Her father.

"Sorry, I don't have what you need here. Might want to head on home," Mr. Ross said and then waved his hand like he'd just dismissed her. Right before the brush-off came a warning look so fast she almost missed it.

Head on home? Was this man serious? Based on his lackluster expression, he was. Giving up on the only lead Emerson had was unimaginable. The hard lines on Mr. Ross's face told her that he wasn't one to give in once he dug his heels in. To prove the point, he started flipping through the pages of the magazine again. Small towns were known for taking care of their own. Was her mother from here? Did she grow up in Cider Creek? Was she still here? If she was, would she want to meet her daughter?

An awareness of the other person in the small building who was walking up right behind her drew her attention away from Mr. Ross. A woodsy and spicy all-male scent filled her senses when she inhaled, causing a low-burning fire to start in her belly.

"May I help you?" Mr. Ross looked over her head at the customer standing behind her. She sidestepped to allow passage as she noticed how wide Mr. Ross's eyes had become.

"Rory Hayes? Is that you all grown up?" he asked.

"Yes, sir." A strong male voice sent sensual vibrations skittering across her skin. And…awareness.

Emerson risked a glance at the tall, handsome-as-sin stranger. He was taller than Mr. Ross by a good two inches, younger by several decades and clearly more attractive. There were big expressive eyes on a face of hard planes with a dimpled chin. He had enough scruff on his face to be sexy. His hair was cut almost military short. A scar on his right cheekbone and rough hands suggested he performed manual labor. The Hayes name sounded familiar, but she couldn't really recall why.

Ignoring the heartbeat that was currently battering inside her rib cage, she unwittingly locked gazes with the stranger. An emotion passed behind those brown eyes of his that she couldn't quite pinpoint, but she could stare into those honey-browns for days.

"Are you home to stay?" Mr. Ross asked. The man seemed a little too ready for a distraction.

"Visiting," Rory stated. His tone had that polite but impatient edge that Mr. Ross seemed blissfully unaware of. Or maybe the older man was trying to force conversation with Rory so she would give up and leave. Since all her hopes of figuring out who the woman in the picture could be were pinned on Bynum Ross, she stayed rooted to the spot. Maybe she could wait him out and he'd get so tired of her standing there that he would give her some piece of information. Anything would be better than what she'd walked in the door with.

"How long has it been?" Bynum asked.

"Almost thirteen years." After he swiped his card and while waiting for his receipt, Rory stared at the picture that was still on the counter. He turned to her. The air in the room crackled the second their eyes met.

"I grew up here and still know a few folks in town. I'll be around a couple of days and don't mind asking around if you need a hand," he said.

Those words sounded like heaven. Did she dare

hope this man could help find her mother? If so, was Emerson headed toward another reality slap?

"THAT'S NOT NECESSARY," Bynum Ross interjected in a surprise move to Rory. In fact, he couldn't figure out why the older man cared at all.

"I just heard you saying that you couldn't help," Rory pointed out. "Now, I might have been gone a long time, but last I checked, folks in ranching communities still helped each other out. Or has something changed I don't know about?"

The stranger blinked a couple of times like she couldn't believe her ears. A twinge of guilt hit Rory. He hadn't been home in twelve years. Had Cider Creek changed so much that he could no longer recognize it? Bynum still owned the bait and tackle shop, so, clearly, not everything was different.

"Emerson," she said, turning to him and offering what could only be described as long delicate fingers in a surprisingly firm handshake.

"Rory Hayes," he said before shooting Bynum a look. "What's going on?"

"I didn't say anything was." Bynum seemed to backpedal as he threw his hands out. "This young lady is mistaken. No one here can help with what she's asking. That's all. There's no need to waste her time when she probably has better things to do."

Bynum had never been one to speak unnecessarily. The fact he was babbling didn't sit well with

Rory. Meant he was either covering up something or lying. The question was why.

"The 'young lady' probably has a good handle on what she wants to ask and why," Rory defended. "I'm sure she has her reasons that have nothing to do with any one of us. But if we can help her, we should. That's all I'm saying."

"Suit yourself," Bynum said with a shrug. And yet, his stiff shoulders belied the sense of ease he was trying to portray.

Again, why?

What could Bynum possibly have to gain from dismissing Emerson? Rory was curious now and he was in no rush to get home anyway.

"It's okay," Emerson said before turning to Bynum, who pulled a handkerchief out of his pocket and blotted the small beads of sweat that had formed on his upper lip. Interesting that the older man could be sweating considering it was fifty-eight degrees outside last time Rory checked the thermometer in his truck.

His cell buzzed. He fished it out of his pocket and checked the screen.

"I need to take this," Rory said by way of apology as he started toward the door. "I'll be back to get my things."

"Go ahead. They'll be waiting right here," Bynum said. The sense of relief in his voice sent up another red flag but Rory had to take this call. He made a beeline for the door before answering. He could call

Liv back if she rolled into voicemail but he couldn't risk anyone in town finding out he had a daughter before his mother heard the news. He would be in trouble either way but there was no use making it worse.

Outside, he immediately answered and caught the call in time.

"Hey, kiddo," he said. "What's up?"

"Hi, Daddy," Liv practically chirped. On the cusp of her thirteenth birthday, his once sweet and innocent child was morphing into a teenager complete with the emotional ups and downs to prove it. He never knew what her mood was going to be. Based on her tone, she was having a good day.

"How was school today?" he asked, glancing back through the glass doors in time to see Bynum coming around the counter at Emerson. With his index finger, Bynum poked the newcomer in the middle of the chest. *Whoa.*

"It was good," Liv said, interrupting his train of thought before starting into a detailed exposition about her friends Rachel and Dirk, who had apparently got into yet another verbal sparring match in the lunchroom. Liv sighed heavily. "Now no one wants to sit together and I'm supposed to decide which one of my friends I like the most. It's insane, Dad. Like, how am I supposed to deal with them when they won't speak to each other?"

"I'm sure they'll work out their differences," he reassured. In truth, Rory couldn't remember what he'd been like at twelve years old, but the word *hand-*

ful came to mind, especially considering he had five brothers. *Rowdy* was another word that probably fit the bill. He and his brothers had been close growing up, which caused another pang of guilt at the fact they'd grown so far apart. Most didn't even know they were uncles.

Friendships were everything to Liv at this stage.

"I highly doubt it," she protested. He'd also noticed how dramatic she'd become in the past year and feared it was only ramping up.

"Can I call you back in a few minutes?" he asked. Liv didn't seem to have anything critical to report or discuss, and he very much wanted to go back inside to find out what the hell Bynum's problem was. He'd been a longtime friend of Rory's father. They'd been close enough for him to attend a few barbecues every summer. The man was going too far as he backed Emerson up a couple of steps, and Rory couldn't idly stand by.

"Sure, Dad," Liv whined. She really was a great kid and he hoped he was doing a good job with her. Being a single parent was not for the faint of heart, and he'd been a kid himself when she'd been born.

"Or we could keep talking," he offered. Without a partner around to help bring up Liv, everything was on him. All he wanted was for his daughter to be healthy, grow up happy and figure out what she wanted to do in life—the same as every other parent. At least he guessed others wanted the same things. He'd never had the time to join any parent groups as he'd been busy building a home construction business from the ground up.

"I'd love to, Dad, but Rachel's calling, so I better go. Love you," Liv said and immediately ended the call before he had a chance to respond.

This encounter summed up life with an almost teenager. She needed him until she didn't. But what had his attention right now was the way Bynum was treating Emerson. Blame his upbringing or the fact chivalry wasn't dead in his book, but he couldn't watch a person being intimidated by someone bigger or louder.

He might regret his actions, but that didn't stop him from marching back inside.

"What the hell, Bynum?" Rory asked.

"Mind your business, son." Bynum's words shot right through Rory.

This was his business now and he intended to keep at it until Bynum gave an acceptable answer.

Chapter Two

"Sorry for the intrusion. I'm on my way out," Emerson said as she faced off Bynum Ross. His anger told her that he knew more than he was willing to say. The situation was frustrating to say the least, and she wasn't making any ground in getting him to speak up. In fact, staying longer only pushed her further away from the truth.

The fact Bynum knew something and wasn't speaking gave her the confidence to know she was on the right track. It also made her aware that the subject of her mother was touchy for some folks. Her dad? She was scratching her head there because he was the last person she'd expected to lie to her about something so important. Ralph Bennett had been a good father to her. He'd dropped her off at school every morning on his way to work. He'd worked hard to provide for them, and she'd never been without food or a roof over her head. There'd always been clothes on her back. Her father had been conservative in the way he'd wanted her to dress, but that seemed to come with the territory when it came to fathers. Emerson's best friend, Anna, had complained about her parents plenty of times when it came to clothing.

Growing up without a mother had been tough on Emerson. But that was the past.

Now all she could think about was why hers had been kept from her and whose face was it in the pictures hanging on the walls...because she now knew it hadn't been her birth mother.

Was she adopted? That was one of half a dozen questions flooding her thoughts. And it was apparent Bynum Ross knew something but had no plans to come clean.

Emerson would find out who the woman in the picture was without him. Because his reaction already told her that she was on the right track.

"Are you sure you don't want to stick around and talk this out?" Rory asked. The offer was tempting but she knew when she'd lost a fight. She needed to retreat to her corner so she could regroup and come at it from a different angle.

"No, thanks," she said. "I need to check in to my room anyway. It'll be dark soon and I'm new in town, so I better get going."

It was a white lie because she didn't technically have a room. After this encounter, she planned to get one. Sticking around in Cider Creek for a couple of days would be worth it if she could find out the identity of the woman in the photo.

"Mind if I walk you out to your car?" Rory asked.

"Not at all," she stated. Under normal circumstances, she wouldn't accept an offer from a near stranger. There was something about Rory Hayes that put her at ease when she normally ran the other way from people.

Bynum's face dropped.

"You sure you want to get involved?" he asked Rory as he leaned over the counter.

"Do you mind bagging my stuff?" Rory asked, avoiding answering while motioning toward the cash register. Her respect for Rory was growing by the minute. He admitted to being gone for years, so she wasn't sure how helpful he could be. On the plus side, the picture of her mother was from a long time ago. Maybe he would remember something that could lead to a different trail than this one.

Could she go to the sheriff? The thought hadn't occurred to her until now. Based on Bynum Ross's reaction to her, she wondered if the sheriff might be a better avenue. If asking around brought up the kinds of emotions she'd just seen in the shop owner, then she should probably bring in law enforcement just to keep it safe. But to do what? To say what?

Emerson needed dinner and a fresh cup of coffee so she could better think this through. Coming here, she hadn't known what to expect at B-T or from Bynum Ross. Although she hadn't expected to be welcomed with open arms, Bynum's reaction to her added to the list of questions she had about her mother and the circumstances by which she'd come to give her daughter away.

"Whatever you say," Bynum said to Rory as the older man reclaimed his spot behind the counter. His complexion reddened and his gaze narrowed as he rang up the couple of items on the counter before giving a total for Rory's purchases.

Emerson couldn't wait to leave the bait shop after the encounter with its owner. There were too many competing ideas rolling around in her thoughts. Too many fears being stirred up based on his reaction. She hovered by the door, waiting for Rory as requested. At this point, she would take any lead she could get considering the one name she had just fizzled out, refusing to give her any information and warning her not to dig around. The warning still sent an icy chill down her back.

Going home empty-handed wasn't an option.

Rory joined her at the door after paying for his items. She pushed the door open, and he followed her outside.

"Thank you for your kindness in there," she said, motioning toward the building as she stopped in front of her bright orange Bronco.

"I don't know what that was about," Rory said. "But I promise this town is friendlier than that. Or at least it was."

"You don't live here anymore," she said.

He shook his head.

"I've been gone a long time," he said without offering the details.

"Your last name sounds familiar," she said, cocking an eyebrow.

He half smiled, half sighed.

"We're known for being a cattle ranching family," he stated. "Bynum used to be a friend of my father's when he was alive."

"I'm sorry for your loss," she said, remembering the dozens of times those same words had been spoken to her in recent weeks.

Rory shrugged it off like it was nothing, but the emotion that passed behind his eyes told a different story. He seemed to stifle it before saying, "I appreciate it. Still tough even though it's been a year."

The subject was now closed if the way he clamped his mouth shut was any indication.

"My father passed away recently," she offered, thinking it wouldn't hurt to share a little about herself. "It's been a couple of weeks now and I was going through his things when I found the picture that apparently upset Mr. Ross." She left out the part where she was trying to track down a woman who might not want anything to do with Emerson. Not all folks wanted to be found. Based on Bynum's reaction to Emerson, her mother might be one of them.

"I'm truly sorry. Losing a parent is never easy," Rory said with warmth and compassion in his voice. "Were the two of you close?"

"I thought so," she admitted. "He did the best he could raising me on his own."

The nod and resignation in his eyes registered with her. Kindred spirit? Should she ask him about it? After studying him for a long moment, she decided not to press. If he wanted to share, he would. She would leave it at that. For reasons she didn't want to examine, she glanced down at his ring finger. A sense of relief she had no right to own washed over her when she noticed it was bare.

"How long was it just the two of you?" he asked.

"For as long as I can remember," she admitted. "He was a good dad, don't get me wrong. But it could be hard at times."

"Having a son would have made it easier on him, I'm sure," Rory said.

"I can't count the number of times I thought the same thing," she stated. "He loved me, though. And he was protective. I never doubted that he was doing the best he could."

Until now. Until the lies. Until the betrayal.

Now everything she believed she knew about her relationship with her father was suspect.

"Like fathers are when it comes to their little girls," he said, then quickly added, "or so I've heard." She wondered if his father had been the same with him. A father-son relationship seemed like a whole different ball game based on her friends' families.

She figured this was as good a time as any to feel him out about the woman in the picture.

"You already know why I'm here," she stated, trying to control the unexpected rush of emotion at shifting focus to her mother. Emerson's heart hammered her ribs from the inside out, and her pulse raced as she pulled the picture out of her handbag. The print on the edges of the five-by-seven photo were tattered from the separation and a chunk was taken out right next to Emerson's face. Luckily, the woman in the photo who undeniably resembled Emerson was clearly visible. "This is the only picture I have and it's old."

"May I?" Rory asked, holding his hand out. She placed the picture on the flat of his extended palm.

"The writing on the back is too smeared to make out and most of it has rubbed off anyway," she said as he studied the picture. The blue ink was almost completely illegible. When Emerson had tried to broach the subject with her aunt, she'd been shut down faster than a barrel horse after the last turn. Since there was more than one way to find answers, she'd moved on by researching the location of B-T and who the owner was.

The corners of Rory's lips—lips she had to force her gaze away from—turned down in a frown.

"I'm sorry. Can't say I recognize the face based on this picture," he said. "Is she missing?"

"Not exactly," Emerson said, wondering how much of her story it was wise to share with someone she'd met a few minutes ago. There was something easygoing about him that made her want to push herself out of her comfort zone and trust him. She'd realized long ago it had most likely been a mistake to come here in the first place. What did she hope to find? In the best-case scenario, her mother was gone. In the worst case her mother had abandoned Emerson as a baby, not to mention walked out on Emerson's dad. Or perhaps her father had walked out. Had her mother done something terrible enough to result in that?

For the first time since finding the photo and over-hearing her aunt's whispers, Emerson asked herself if she really wanted to know the answer. Could she handle the truth, or would it just kick up a dust storm of emotions? Sadness? Betrayal by the one person who was supposed to love and protect her? Maybe she should walk away and leave it alone. Because pursuing this could uncover a path of deception by her father. At least he *was* her father. She'd been able to use a hair sample from his hairbrush to confirm a DNA match. She wouldn't have to search missing kid files to find out the truth. But he'd hidden the identity of her mother. As much as she wished she could walk away and forget all about it, her brain didn't work that way.

Nonetheless, she decided it was best not to give out too much information about the photo and better to see what others knew before she shared her life story.

"I'm trying to track down and reach out to rela-tives to notify them of my father's passing," she said on a shrug. "This woman isn't truly a missing person—she's just missing to me."

Emerson glanced up and was met with the most beautiful and sympathetic pair of honey-brown eyes.

"Families are interesting," he stated with the kind of compassion that said he had his own struggles with family.

"Mind if I ask where you're staying in case I get any information?" he asked.

"Based on what? A description?" she asked.

"I was thinking that I could snap a pic using my phone," he stated.

"Right. Good idea," she said, figuring she was going to have to trust him a little if she wanted help.

He pulled out his phone—a phone that seemed to be lighting up with text messages. Someone seemed in serious need of being in contact with him…a girlfriend or a wife? The thought probably shouldn't make her shoulders sag or her chest deflate.

He snapped the pic and then palmed his cell. Was he hiding something? It seemed the whole world had a secret.

"I'll ask around and see what kind of response I get. My mother or Granny might know something," he said on a shrug. His cell buzzed and he took a step back as he glanced at the screen. Then came, "Work call."

A telltale sign this most likely was a personal call instead came when he walked away to answer. A man this intensely good-looking probably had a whole bevy of women waiting in the wings for a chance to spend time with him. He didn't strike her as the kind of person who would welcome the attention, so it caught her off guard that she'd pegged him wrong. Because he'd already had one private call a little while ago when they were inside the bait shop and now a second.

Too bad. But then, she wasn't in Cider Creek to find a date.

While Rory was preoccupied with his back turned to her, Emerson slipped into her Bronco and quietly closed the door. He was so engaged in conversation that he didn't so much as glance her way when she fired up the engine. She could pull over and search the internet on her phone for a place to stay once she got away from the bait and tackle shop.

When she glanced in the rearview mirror as she pulled out of the parking she saw the shop owner was on a call, standing almost pressed against the glass. A creepy-crawly feeling traveled over her skin as she pressed the gas pedal.

Based on Bynum's tense body posture, she'd opened a can of worms.

"I HAVE TO GO," Rory told his office manager and right hand Cecile Welch. "Check on Liv for me?"

"You betcha," Cecile said, but all the usual cheerfulness was out of her tone on this call.

"Keep me posted on what the fire marshal has to say about the house," he stated, wondering if this day could get any worse. He'd already made the drive down from DFW, where he'd built a successful home building company, to face the music at home. For over a dozen years, he'd been dreading the day he would make this particular trip. And now one of his new builds that had just been drywalled had a small fire. It happened on construction sites from time to time, but he didn't like it. Then there was the strange way Bynum was acting. The only bright spot had been meeting Emerson. He genuinely hoped to help her find the woman in the picture.

Speaking of Emerson, when he'd turned around to ask for her number in case he was able to dig up useful information, she was gone. The Bronco that had been parked on the other side of the building had disappeared.

As he turned toward his truck, he saw Bynum out of the corner of his eye. His grandfather's old acquaintance backed away from the glass window as the lights came on in the store. This time of year, it got dark before suppertime. But the look on Bynum's face said trouble was brewing.

Rory was too late to warn Emerson. He'd failed to get her cell number. Of course, there was only one decent place to stay anywhere near town, Bluebonnet Bed and Breakfast. The place was owned by the Randolph family, if that was still true after all these years. Bynum was different to the point Rory didn't recognize the man any longer. Granted, his physical description was the same other than the obvious fact he'd aged, but that was where the similarities stopped. A thought niggled at the back of Rory's mind. Bynum had been close with Rory's grandfather. If Bynum was involved in the disappearance of the woman in the picture, he couldn't help but to wonder if his own grandfather might have been involved as well. At this point, Rory wouldn't put anything past his grandfather, as sad as the fact was. The man had proved he'd do anything to protect his own reputation.

All his warning systems flared when he heard the sound of a truck barreling down the farm road. Folks didn't usually speed at or after sundown so they wouldn't risk hitting a deer. The driver was going fast enough to get Rory's attention.

Hands on his hips, he stood there and watched as the truck blew by. And he immediately realized Emerson was in danger.

Chapter Three

A pair of headlights on high beam roared up behind Emerson. Was this jerk seriously going to whip around her on this two-lane farm road at night? Texas drivers were known for being aggressive, but this was extreme.

Also, what was up with the headlights? Annoyed, she decided this wasn't the battle she needed to fight. She had no plans to upset an aggressive driver further when this person was clearly in a mood.

Rather than hog the road, she shifted as far as possible to the right shoulder, making it that much easier for the vehicle to pass her. The driver had other ideas. The truck made the move right along with her as if connected by an invisible tether.

A shot of adrenaline pulsed through her, causing her hands to tremble as she tightened her grip on the steering wheel. Her first thought was the driver had to be drunk, but yet there was no weaving or carelessness. His movements were controlled and intentional. Was she just in the wrong place at the wrong time, or was someone targeting her? But who would do such a thing?

Bynum Ross.

Bynum had not received her well, his reaction caused the tiny hairs on the back of her neck to stand up. She studied her rearview mirror, but the blinding high beams shot any chance of her getting a good look at the driver.

Emerson swerved over into the empty lane for oncoming traffic. The truck immediately followed suit, sending an icy chill racing down her spine. The driver was following her moves exactly. And then a second set of headlights came into view from farther behind the truck.

This can't be good.

Truck number one roared up and then clipped her bumper on the driver's side, sending her into a tailspin. She yanked the wheel, turning into the spin and then back out as the tires struggled for purchase as she fishtailed.

The blare of a horn behind them rent the air. Her tires gained traction, and she maneuvered out of the spin without flipping the Bronco—a small miracle. Now, out of the spin, she navigated off the paved road where she hoped the truck couldn't follow.

The terrain was bumpy, and she was jostled all around inside the vehicle. Her head jerked to the right and back, whiplashed. There were no streetlights on the farm road, so she had to rely on her own headlights. High beams gave her a broader viewpoint, but the terrain caused her to drastically slow her speed. All Emerson wanted to do was put as much distance between her and the trucks as possible. The front end of her Bronco dipped on the passenger side. She bit back a curse and slammed on the brakes.

For a split second, she focused on the rearview mirror. Was the truck coming for her? A second was all it took for the front end of her Bronco to smack into a tree when she veered off course slightly to the right.

The jolt deployed her side and front airbags, cushioning her body from the blow. The sudden stop shook her to the core, and it took a second for her brain to catch up to what had just happened. Shock robbed her voice as she tried to scream.

Where was her purse? Her cell phone?

She fumbled around for the seat belt release, found it. Another second later, she scrambled to find her handbag, which had been sitting in the passenger seat unsecured. The purse's contents were scattered all over the floorboard and underneath the seat. The bag was probably somewhere on the floorboard too.

It was dark behind the Bronco so there were no headlights coming toward her at least. The bit of good news didn't exactly warm her insides. She was vulnerable alone in a strange town.

What the hell had she been thinking coming here half-cocked with no idea of what she might be facing? If her own father had gone to great lengths to hide the identity of her mother, there must have been a good reason. Her heart squeezed thinking about him. He clearly had been trying to protect her from the truth. Why? Did her mother do something wrong? Illegal? Was she some kind of addict? A drunk? Criminal?

She'd had no idea what kind of people to expect in Cider Creek. Arlington was a large enough city to behave like one; neighbors didn't know each other unless they'd lived in a home for most of their lives, a rare occurrence. In a small town, she'd expected folks to be friendly.

Of course, it would be a whole lot easier if she could go straight to the source. Not being able to ask her father or get answers directly from him broke Emerson's heart. She would never be able to hear his side of the story. The crushing thought threatened to crack her chest in half as the reality sunk in. Her father was gone.

Tears pricked the backs of Emerson's eyes. Grief was odd. There were so many times throughout the day when Emerson believed she would be fine, able to deal with her new reality. And then something would happen, or a memory would come to her out of the blue that reminded her of the fact he'd died. She was an orphan now. No mother. No father.

She blinked away the pools forming in her eyes, blurring her vision. Where was that damn cell phone anyway?

Sprawled across the seats, her fingers stretched to the limit, she touched something that resembled the shape of her phone. Emerson inched a little closer and reached for it. The screen was so cracked the likelihood of her phone being useful was nil. She tried anyway.

And then she heard the heavy thunder of footsteps coming toward her.

Voice. She could speak and ask for 911.

"Emerson," the familiar voice whispered. Rory? What was he doing here? A burst of relief erupted in her chest.

"Yes. Here. Inside the Bronco," she whispered back.

"Help is on the way," he said as he approached the passenger side. Emerson was grateful to the airbags, which had most likely saved her life, and she was even more so to the stranger who cared enough to come to her rescue. It dawned on her that he'd been driving the car with the second set of headlights. Had he sensed that she was in danger? The other truck would have had to have passed right by him.

The door handle jiggled as his face came into view in the window, but it didn't open. The crash on that side must have jammed the door, even though the front-side bumper took the impact.

Rory appeared on the driver's side of the vehicle. After a couple of hard jerks, the door came flying open and her gaze immediately dropped to the shotgun resting in the crook of his arm.

"Are you badly injured?" he asked, assessing her as he kept an eye trained on the field around them.

Her instincts said she could trust him. He was there to help.

"Not that I know of," she admitted. Nothing hurt more than expected, although she could be in shock. She could move all her limbs. Her fingers worked. She'd been conscious the whole time. "Do you know who was driving the truck?"

"No idea," he said. "Any visible bleeding?"

"I don't think so," she said, hoping it was true. In her haste to grab her phone and call for help, she hadn't taken stock of any possible injuries. She checked the mirror and didn't see any nose bleeds, scrapes, or contusions anywhere. Everything seemed to be working all right so far. Thank heavens it wasn't worse.

For the first time she believed she might actually survive this ordeal thanks to her guardian angel.

Rory Hayes.

A SENSE OF relief washed over Rory like few he'd experienced in his lifetime. Emerson was alive and talking. He had no idea what Bynum Ross was doing but had every intention of finding out. First, he needed to make certain Emerson was out of the woods medically and the two of them were safe. The driver of the truck might still be out there.

"I requested the law and an ambulance," Rory said to Emerson. The instant he'd caught sight of her splayed out across the front seat, the worst had come to mind. Erasing the image and the fear that came along with it would take effort. "Can you move okay?"

"Yes." She twisted around until she was sitting up in the driver's seat. It was all he could do not to pull her into an embrace and offer to be her comfort. Touching her might be a bad idea. In fact, her moving at all before she was checked out by an EMT was a bad idea, but it was too late now.

"Let's stay right here until help arrives," he said. She might've been hurting more than she was letting on. Being out here like sitting ducks for the driver of the truck sat hard in his gut.

With one hand, he managed to turn on the flashlight app on his cell phone. He stepped into the door in order to hold it open with his body as he scanned the area around them. He couldn't see more than an eight-foot radius around him, which worried him. His own truck was still on the road and he could see his emergency flashers in the distance.

"You'll get no argument from me," she said. "Is he gone?"

"I think so," he said but had very little reassurance to offer. It was worrisome the driver of the other truck could still be around somewhere in the shadows. Or might have dropped off a passenger, who was currently stalking them like prey. There were a whole lot of good hunters in this area. A skilled shooter with a long-range rifle could pick them both off at a distance. Fortunately, they had the Bronco to provide some type of cover.

"Did the 911 operator say how long it would be before someone arrived?" she asked, and he could hear the shakiness in her voice. She was most likely in shock and pumped full of adrenaline. From the glow of the flashlight app, he could see that her pupils were dilated. It wasn't freezing outside but her body shivered—another sign of shock and the effects of adrenaline.

"Twenty minutes, give or take," he said, which meant they were on their own until then.

A twig snapped to his right. He spun toward the sound as he lifted the barrel of the shotgun.

"Shine the light when I say," he instructed, slipping his phone into Emerson's hand and using the Bronco as cover. The instant their fingers grazed a jolt of electricity shot through him. This wasn't the time to analyze the unfamiliar zing.

Rory listened carefully as he watched and waited. Patience and timing were the name of the game, and he had every intention of getting off the first shot.

Chapter Four

To say Emerson might have stirred up a hornet's nest seemed like an understatement if the truck had intentionally run her off the road. Targeted her? Those scary words might be her new reality. A growing piece of her wanted to run home to Arlington and put this behind her. The odds her mother actually wanted to meet Emerson seemed slim based on the fact the woman hadn't tried to contact her daughter once in almost thirty years as far as Emerson knew. With social media, it wasn't exactly difficult to find someone unless they were hiding.

Now that Emerson was in Cider Creek asking questions, she'd experienced what it was like to hit a brick wall named Bynum Ross and a literal tree with her Bronco. All in all, it had been a red-letter day so far. She couldn't say the six-hour drive had been worth it considering she was no closer to figuring out her mother's identity. To add insult to injury, her front bumper was banged up and her vehicle in need of repair. She had no idea how much that was going to cost her. Emerson wasn't rich. The small estate her father had left wasn't much, and it'd be a year clearing probate.

As far as Emerson knew, she was his next of kin. There weren't more children out there to come collect on her father's estate. To hear her aunt speak, Emerson's mother might turn up claiming she deserved a piece of the pie. Would a woman who'd abandoned her child—only child?—come asking for money?

Emerson couldn't say one way or the other. She would have to know a person before she could make a judgment about them.

The noise must have come from a wild animal. One that might have stalked and killed her if she'd been left to her own devices out here while waiting for a tow truck. An involuntary shiver rocked her body at the thought of the many creepy-crawlies around here that could feast on her. Most of the creatures in her hometown were found in a building behind a glass at a terrarium or in captivity at a nature center. Arlington was squarely in between Dallas and Fort Worth in the DFW metroplex. Dallas was more of a metropolitan city than outsiders gave it credit for being, and Fort Worth was working hard to shed its Cowtown image to become a foodie destination in addition to being a booming tourist attraction for its stockyards. Emerson usually told out-of-towners she ate more sushi in Dallas than steak, and the city was a shopping mecca.

"It's probably nothing," Rory finally concluded after a few tense minutes that seemed to drag on. He lowered the barrel of the shotgun, keeping the trigger close enough to pull off a quick shot.

"Any idea who that was?" She knew full well he hadn't been around town in years, but her impression of small towns was that they didn't change much. This line of thinking was the reason she'd rolled the dice and come here in the first place. The reasoning might be flawed, considering she had zip for experience to back her up. And yet she had to believe that if her mother had been from Cider Creek or lived here any length of time, someone would remember. Bynum's reaction to seeing Emerson reinforced the notion. The hint of recognition in his eyes caused her to believe he'd been hiding information. It did occur to her that she might have been seeing what she wanted to see.

"Afraid not," he said on a frustrated-sounding sigh. "I know I've already said this once, but Cider Creek has always been a nicer town than what you're being shown right now. Folks here usually come to each other's aid, not cause the problem in the first place."

"How do you know what the town is like if you haven't been back in...how long did you say?" She cocked her head to one side, curious as to why he'd come to her rescue again.

"Nearly thirteen years," he supplied. "And you're

right. I don't know. Once I left town, I didn't look back."

"Mind if I ask why?"

"Personal problems, I guess," he said on a shrug that would convince no one.

"None you care to discuss with a stranger," she said, figuring she might as well speak her mind.

"That's right," he said.

"Personal problems brought me to town," she said. For the second time today, she wondered if she'd made the right call in coming here. Maybe some secrets should stay buried. What if she ended up with a rare medical condition and needed to know her mother's health history in order for treatment to work? The thought had crossed her mind now that she couldn't trust anything her father had told her. If he'd lied about her family tree…what else had he covered up?

"Families can be tricky to navigate," Rory said with the kind of conviction that told her there was a story behind those words.

"Amen to that." She glanced around as the chirps grew louder in the distance. Cicadas? Crickets? She couldn't tell the difference. As long as they stayed in the woods and she stuck to the road, they'd all get along just fine. "Thank you, in case I didn't adequately express my gratitude yet."

He tipped his Stetson.

"Ma'am," he said. That one word sent sensual shivers racing up her arms.

As much as she didn't like being called a word that made her want to look over her shoulder for her aunt, she knew he meant it in a good way. Besides, with a deep timbre like his, he could make reading the ingredients from a cereal box come off as sexy.

"Were you headed this way?" she asked, wondering if his showing up was coincidence or something else.

"No," he admitted. "I saw the truck come barreling past the bait shop a few minutes after you'd left. I also noticed Bynum was on the phone, standing at the window and looking that way. He seemed worked up back at the store for no reason, not to mention being flat-out rude to a newcomer. The whole incident has been sticking in my craw. I got a bad feeling when the truck whizzed past me, so I hopped in my truck and headed this way."

"I'm grateful you did." She couldn't imagine what might have happened if he hadn't scared off the driver.

"Plus, what could Bynum possibly have against you for searching for a woman in an old photograph?" he continued after a nod of acknowledgment.

"That's the question of the hour, isn't it?" she asked, but the question was rhetorical and he seemed to know it.

"Doesn't add up," he said.

"Not in my book, either," she agreed. "Unless the woman in the picture did something to him years ago that he's never been able to let go of. Or possibly hurt someone in this town. Someone he cared about." She paused for a couple of beats. "From what I gather, she abandoned me, so I have no idea what kind of person I'm trying to find."

"The woman in the picture is your mother?" His eyebrow shot up with the question. "I thought I saw a resemblance but wasn't sure what kind of relative we were talking about here."

"It's difficult to call her by that, but the short answer is yes," she said. "At least, I believe so."

"And you're here to find the truth," he summed up as an emotion passed behind his eyes that she couldn't quite pinpoint.

"That's right."

He brought his hand up to rub the day-old scruff on his chin. It looked like he was about to ask a question and then seemed to think better of it.

"Is your family expecting you?" She figured asking wouldn't do any harm.

"At some point," he said. "I told them I'd come home but I didn't give a whole lot of details." He clamped his mouth shut like he was about to say something else.

A pair of headlights in the distance caused her to flinch. Rory checked his cell phone.

"It's the law," he said. "Deputy Theodore Harlingen."

"I should probably get busy calling a tow truck," she said as she came around to the front of her Bronco. "The fender doesn't look good and I probably shouldn't drive her again until I know for sure everything is good to go." Emerson retrieved her cell phone from her purse. "I need to grab an Uber."

Rory cracked a small smile.

"Where did you say you were from?" he asked.

"Arlington," she supplied.

"Last I checked, there weren't a whole lot of car services in Cider Creek," he said. "You might be waiting a long time if you're trying to use an app to get a ride."

"Maybe a tow truck driver can give me a ride," she said. "I'll just google one—"

"I already made a call," Rory interrupted, "but I can cancel if you'd rather do it yourself."

Reality dawned that she was alone in this. Should she continue to accept help from a stranger even though he'd proved that he wasn't out to hurt her? What the hell? Right now, she could use a friend like Rory.

"Plus, I can give you a ride wherever you need to go." Rory didn't want to admit to himself how much he wanted her to take him up on the offer. Of course, it might be guilt taking the wheel. He'd kept his daughter a secret from the family, except for his older brother Callum, for twelve years running. Did his mother have the right to know about her granddaughter? Was Liv missing out because she only had him to depend on?

Technically, she had Callum too. His brother had

been sworn to secrecy. He'd proved that he could be trusted too even though Rory was one hundred percent certain his brother didn't approve of keeping the secret this long. To be fair, he hadn't intended for any of this to happen. Duncan Hayes had made it clear to Rory that he wasn't having any bastard children running around on the ranch he'd worked his whole life to build. The older man had made it clear as a bell that Rory had betrayed the family with the accidental pregnancy and would bring shame to the Hayes name if he kept the child. After moving north to Mesquite and working his tail end off to make ends meet, Liv's mother had said they were too young to bring up a child. Rory had argued otherwise. Leah Grove packed up her things and wished him good luck.

He'd never understood how a parent could walk away from her own flesh and blood like Leah had. She'd claimed a baby was too hard. Yeah? Life was hard. Didn't mean quitting was the right thing to do.

So, he'd worked double time to care for his little girl and he'd worked his hide off to give her the life she deserved without spoiling her. But no matter how well he did, there was always a thought niggling at the back of his mind as to whether or not he'd been unfair to his mother by not telling her about Liv.

At eighteen, he'd been easier to influence. His grandfather was impenetrable. His claims about Rory bringing shame to his mother had struck a nerve. Rory convinced himself he'd done the right thing by leaving and cutting off contact with his family. His grandfather had said it would be better this way anyway. But how long was too long to stay away? Now that Rory was older, he second-guessed the decision to leave town. It almost felt like he'd cowered.

Was offering help to Emerson his way of proving that he wasn't a bad person? He'd given a whole lot of money to charity in recent years. He'd built homes pro bono for single parent families. None of those acts filled the hole in his chest at wondering if Marla Hayes deserved to know she had a grandchild.

The deputy pulled alongside them. He was followed by a tow truck and an EMT.

"Rory? Is that seriously you?" Theodore Harlingen asked.

"Theo? When did you become a deputy?" Rory asked, shocked that one of his old high school buddies had chosen to uphold the law. To be fair, they'd all been good kids. They played the occasional prank. Went skinny-dipping in Ghost Lake during hot summers. But that was the extent of their criminal activity unless he counted all the merciless teasing over the years.

"Been a few years now," Theo said as he exited his vehicle. He offered a firm handshake.

"Why did I expect time to freeze while I was away?" Rory asked as Jimmy Zenon walked up after exiting his tow truck.

"Jimmy took over his family's business," Theo explained. Rory resented that he felt guilty for not having done the same thing, because when he was eighteen years old and in desperate need of help, no hand up had been offered by his grandfather. In fact, Rory had been pressured to leave town with his tail tucked between his legs. Rory and his girlfriend had dated all through high school. Looking back, they'd been barely more than children except it hadn't felt that way when they'd turned eighteen, legal adults. He'd been naive enough to believe they were both in it for the long haul, so taking the next step in their four-year relationship had seemed like the most natural thing.

"Rory Hayes?" Jimmy made a show of rubbing his eyes. "Can't be. That boy left town ages ago. There's a grown man standing in front of me now." Jimmy walked over until he stood almost toe-to-toe with Rory, then looked him up, down and sideways.

"Don't you look the same even after all these years," Rory said to Jimmy, giving him a playful shove to force him back a step. "Did you hit puberty yet? I can't tell."

Jimmy chuckled.

"Any day now," he said with a smile that ran ear to ear. Then he jabbed Rory in the shoulder. The light tap brought Rory back to their high school days when the punches had been harder and their intelligence victim to their raging hormones. He'd swear he gained fifteen IQ points once he finally got out of puberty. His decisions, he admitted, had gotten a whole lot better too.

"You took over for your dad?" Rory asked, but it was more statement than question.

"Yeah," Jimmy said. "Family is everything. Right? Got to take care of our own."

Rory nodded.

"How's Leah, by the way?" Jimmy asked. He must not have looked for a ring.

"I wouldn't know." Rory left it at that. He didn't want to go into the details of the breakup. Plus, no one seemed to know about their kid. A small town like Cider Creek prized personal connections and the Wi-Fi was spotty out here anyway, so most folks met up in town to talk. Social media hadn't taken off here in the way it seemed to possess most of the country, and he didn't think a whole lot had changed since he left. Plus, he'd taken great pains to ensure Liv's privacy. He'd offered to give her a thousand dollars a year starting at age ten to eighteen if she stayed off all platforms until her eighteenth birthday, payable on her eighteenth birthday. Leah was allowed full access to her daughter, not that she ever took him up on the offer all those years ago. She hadn't contacted him since and he assumed she wanted to put the whole event behind her and move on.

There were questions dancing in Emerson's eyes, but his past relationship and subsequent daughter were secrets he had to keep.

Chapter Five

"Tell me what happened here," Theo said as he turned toward the crash site.

"A truck came barreling up behind me," Emerson began as the deputy took out his cell phone and began snapping pictures from different angles.

She had no idea how close either of these two were to Bynum Ross. Judging from the way they interacted with each other and Rory, the residents of Cider Creek were tight-knit. She had no idea how they would react to accusations against one of their own if Bynum had orchestrated the scare.

After going over her story one detail at a time, she glanced over at Rory. Tension lines scored his forehead and his hands were fisted at his sides. He flexed and released his fingers a couple of times like he was maybe trying to work off some of the tension. The return to his hometown didn't seem to be as warm and fuzzy as he expected and he seemed genuinely caught off guard by Bynum's reaction.

Jimmy's face was set in a scowl and she couldn't

tell if that was good for her or not. For all she knew their families could be close. Theo was the most unreadable, his poker face no doubt a benefit to his occupation.

"What brings you to town?" Theo asked.

For a split second, she debated lying. Survival instincts told her this might be a good time to get out of Dodge and head home before anyone else could try to run her off the road, or worse. She shivered at the thought this could get worse. At some point, she might have to go to the law to find out about her mother, so she figured she might as well go ahead and get it over with.

"I'm looking for my mother," she explained before recounting her run-in with Bynum at B-T. She produced the picture. Since these were classmates of Rory's, she wasn't surprised when no one recognized the woman in the photo. They were too young, but their parents were a different story. She'd hoped the woman in the picture might have visited their homes at one time or another.

"Do you have a name to go on?" Theo asked.

She shook her head. "It sure would make my search a whole lot easier if I did."

"I figured as much, but you'd be surprised at the answers I get sometimes," he admitted. She could only imagine. "Will you be sticking around town once your vehicle gets repaired?"

"Only as long as I need to," she stated. Despite dropping her gaze, she picked up on a small reaction from Rory Hayes. He didn't seem eager to get to his family home, so it was possible he was hoping she would stay longer so he would have an excuse to delay his return. He seemed like the kind of person who grabbed the bull by the horns rather than ducking and hiding so there had to be a good reason behind his hesitation.

"If there's anything I can do to assist you in your search, don't hesitate to reach out." Theo removed a card from his shirt pocket and offered it to her. She took it and tucked it inside her purse as she thanked him. Too bad he hadn't been able to provide any information on the woman in the photo.

"Will do, Deputy," she said before he turned to Rory.

"How about you?" Theo asked. "You got any plans for supper? Maury would love to see the legendary Rory Hayes back in town. Her dad still talks about the shot you made at the buzzer to win state."

"I'm good for tonight," Rory said with a smile that hinted at embarrassment. "I'll try to swing by sometime while I'm in Cider Creek if Maury promises not to bring up ancient history." He laughed like the statement was meant to be a joke but there was a hint of truth there.

"Sounds good," Theo said. "We have a couple of kiddos who have yet to meet the legend."

"It'd be a short conversation," Rory quipped, clearly uncomfortable. "But I'll stop by with a couple of beers real soon."

"Did you get what you needed?" Jimmy asked Theo. "If I'm not home soon, Claudette will tan my hide. It's my turn with the baby while she has margarita night with SueAnne and Bernadette."

"Take it away," Theo said before turning back to Emerson. "Jimmy will drop off your vehicle at his shop in town. Give him your information before he gets out of here or feel free to stop by Jimmy's Tow and Repair first thing in the morning for a quote."

Her heart sank at the thought of the damage to her Bronco. It was her baby and she hated the thought it might be totaled.

"Do what you can to fix her up, okay?" she said to Jimmy.

"I'll go ahead and brag on him because he won't," Theo said. "If it can be fixed, he's the one who can get the job done. If others say it can't be fixed, he'll show 'em how it's really done."

After her reception with Bynum, trusting anyone in Cider Creek was hard. Rory had stood up for her and he seemed to think these two were okay. Besides, she didn't have a whole lot of choices. She looked to Rory for confirmation, and he gave a slight nod in return.

"Do you need a ride?" Theo asked.

"She's got one," Rory interjected before seeming to realize she might not accept one from him. He flashed eyes at her. "If that's okay."

"Sure, I appreciate it." She pulled out her phone.

"I just need to find a place to stay, so I can tell you where to drop me."

"The Bluebonnet B&B is the only decent place around, if memory serves," Rory stated. It popped up first in her search engine.

"It's the only place around," Jimmy said as he reclaimed the driver's seat after finishing hooking up the Bronco. "Unless you want to go up the highway for the Cider Creek Inn which isn't even in town."

One place to stay in the entire town? Arlington wasn't a huge city by some standards, but there were plenty of hotels, motels and everything in between. She was almost afraid to ask about food options. Did they lock all the doors and roll up the streets at seven o'clock? She felt claustrophobic at the thought.

"Bluebonnet B&B it is," she said. It wouldn't be difficult to find her considering she'd be riding the only horse in town. If Bynum Ross wanted to send someone else—if he was responsible for the truck—he wouldn't have far to go.

Jimmy pulled away as Emerson watched her only form of transportation disappear with him. The deputy sat in his vehicle, typing away into the laptop mounted to his dashboard. She hadn't been in town twenty-four hours yet and had already kicked up a bucketload of trouble.

"Ready?" Rory asked, breaking into her thoughts.

"As much as I'll ever be," she said on a sigh as she walked beside him to his truck. He opened the door for her, which was a nice touch. "Thank you for the ride to the B&B, by the way."

"Any chance I can convince you to go out to dinner first?" he asked. It was an unfair question because she sure didn't want to be alone in a new town with no way to get around. Plus, her heart gave a little flip when he asked, which wasn't a distraction she needed at the moment.

Well, maybe she wasn't looking at the situation right. Rory Hayes might be exactly what she needed, a friend. They were in short supply right now.

"Is anything open?" she asked.

"I have no idea anymore." His chuckle was a low rumble from deep in his chest and it stirred up a whole mess of feelings Emerson was trying to avoid.

A FEW TAPS on Rory's cell phone and it looked like Cider Creek Café was still in business, and open. Next door was Bea's Bakery. Both were within walking distance to the B&B.

"I have a real treat in store for you," Rory said to Emerson. Her smile in response caused his heart to gallop like a horse running free. He wanted to give her a break from the hellacious day she'd had so far. The irony she was desperately searching for her lost mother when Liv's mother knew she had a child and couldn't care less wasn't lost on him. He wished there was some way to shield Emerson from the pain she could face when she finally tracked down the person in the photo.

Besides, there were a few other scenarios that could break her heart too. She might locate her mother only to learn the woman had passed away or was an addict of some kind. If she lived in deplorable conditions and refused help, that would be gut-wrenching. Her mother might have moved on and wanted nothing to do with her daughter. She may not get the welcome one would hope for.

Rory had thought about tracking down Leah a half a dozen times to reunite her with twelve-year-old Liv. Right now, a relationship was possible. If Leah waited, he feared she would lose her daughter forever. Believe him when he said his concern was not for Leah. She'd shown her true colors when she walked away from a newborn without looking back. He didn't want the rejection to hurt Liv for the rest of her life. She was already starting to ask questions he couldn't answer. All he knew for certain was the drama meter had ramped up in recent months and his once-amiable kid was turning into the eye-rolling, heavy-sigh queen. Her vocabulary seemed to be shrinking to a few key phrases on repeat.

"How far is the restaurant?" Emerson asked. She was tapping her finger on the door handle.

"About five minutes, give or take," he responded. Opting for small talk over silence, he asked, "What's your favorite kind of food?"

"My go-to favorite is any kind of pizza," she said as the tapping slowed down a few notches. It was a good sign. "Ever been to the state fair?"

"As a matter of fact, I make it a point to go every year." Liv had a countdown to the fair going on the small whiteboard affixed to the back of her bedroom door. She looked forward to their annual trip more than bees liked honey.

"Really?" A note of surprise caused her tone to rise a couple of octaves.

"You don't pin me for the kind of person who likes to have a good time?" he asked, feigning upset.

"No," she quickly countered. "Based on my limited knowledge of you so far, you seem like the type of person who works seven days a week. You might call it six, but you manage to sneak work in on Sundays too."

"Now you're calling me a workaholic," he said with a chuckle.

"Am I wrong?" she asked.

"No, you are not," he admitted.

"You also own your own construction company, which is why I know you give your men Sundays off, but that's probably when you do paperwork," she continued.

"How'd you know I owned my own—"

Before he finished his sentence, she pointed to the RH Construction logo etched into the back window of the truck.

"Right. Busted," he said. "And you're right about me owning the business. How did you figure out that I work seven days a week, though? Or that I do paperwork on Sundays?"

"Those were guesses," she stated. "While you were looking up a place to eat on your phone, I googled your business name. Figured I should know whose vehicle I was getting in."

"Smart," he said. He almost slipped up and said he hoped his daughter was as diligent with her safety. Then again, if this was Liv, he would have warned her not to get in the truck in the first place. Then again, a grown woman's judgment would be a whole lot keener than a twelve-year-old's. He bit his tongue before Liv's name slipped out or any other crucial information that could lead to questions he wasn't prepared to answer. "What else have you found online?"

"You're very successful and shy away from the spotlight," she said. "Your company is on the internet, but you can't be found on social media under your real name at least, so you must value your privacy."

"People have forgotten how attractive it can be not to share every detail of their lives," he said. "Don't you think?"

"I couldn't agree more," she said without hesitation. "I've heard stories of people checking in at restaurants only to come home to find they've been robbed. I rarely ever post on my page anymore."

"It's the highlight reel of someone's life anyway," he said. "I suspect most of what is posted is more fantasy than truth."

"Everyone is a celebrity on social media," she said. "I went back through and checked every person, every face after figuring out some stranger out there was my mother. I imagined that she was using a fake profile to follow me."

Rory couldn't help but think this might be Liv in a few years. She would have questions about the woman who so willingly walked away from her. Questions he didn't look forward to trying to answer.

On the first day of kindergarten, Liv asked why she didn't have a mother like the other kids in class. She'd caught him off guard, and it was one of many times his heart was almost shredded.

"Since you like the state fair, is it safe to say you also like fried foods?" Rory asked.

"Does this place serve chicken-fried steak?" Emerson asked in response to his question.

"Best in the county," he said. Then he added, "Some folks say it's the best in the state."

"Well then, I know what I'm ordering," she said as he parked.

A dark-colored truck was parked down the road in an unlit area where there were no pedestrians or open businesses. He was suspicious. He made a mental note to keep an eye on the situation as he exited the vehicle and came around to the passenger side.

"I didn't realize it until we started talking about food, but I'm actually starving," Emerson admitted. There'd been a lot of stress in the past couple of hours. Her appetite returning meant she was starting to come off the adrenaline rush.

He needed to find a way to warn her to be on

the lookout without making her scared of her own shadow. He wanted her to be aware, not afraid. Her current expression was a mixture of serious and concerned.

Good. She shouldn't let her guard down. And he would figure out a way to tell her that he was afraid the threat wasn't over during their meal.

Chapter Six

Emerson noticed how Rory had looked beyond her instead of at her after parking the truck in the lot at Cider Creek Café. He'd immediately recovered but there'd been something in his eyes that said he didn't like whatever it was he'd been looking at a few seconds before.

A vehicle was parked on the street, too far away to get a good look inside. It might be nothing, which was most likely why he kept quiet. Based on the day's events, it was obvious the small town had changed a lot since he'd left.

After Theo had asked him about Leah, Emerson had discreetly checked his ring finger for a gold band or a tan line. There wasn't one, which didn't necessarily mean there was no wife or girlfriend in the picture. Since she didn't need to be accused of being a home-wrecker, nor did she want to deal with the consequences that come along with such a title, Emerson decided to ask about his relationship status once they sat down.

From the minute she walked inside Cider Creek Café, she felt like she'd come home. A grandmotherly woman with expressive blue eyes and a full head of short, gray hair came around the cash register wearing a frock, an apron and a beaming smile.

"Rory Hayes," she exclaimed as she made a beeline for him then threw her arms around his waist. She couldn't have been more than five feet, two inches. "When did you get back?"

"Officially, I'm not here yet," he said before adding, "and I'd appreciate it if you kept it that way for now."

"I won't tell a soul even though we both know word usually spreads like dry grass fires in a small town," she said as she turned to Emerson. "Polly Spangler."

"Emerson," she said, accepting an enthusiastic handshake.

"My grandson went to school with Rory," Polly said. The older woman could be a dead ringer for Mrs. Claus with less hair. Her spectacles hung on a string of fake pearls.

"How nice." Emerson realized Polly Spangler was the kind of person who probably knew everyone in town. Once she got some food in her stomach, she planned to ask Rory if he thought it was a good idea to break out the picture again. She was a little gunshy considering the last person she'd shown the photograph to had most likely sent a truck to run her off the road.

"Table for two?" Polly practically beamed at Rory.

Everyone she'd encountered so far seemed to put him up on a pedestal. Even Bynum Ross had given Rory somewhat of a warm welcome. It was good to know she hadn't misjudged him. And if he was a serial killer, they'd been seen by enough witnesses to make him think twice about offing her.

Emerson almost laughed at her thoughts. She was hungry and tired, not the best combination for thinking straight. Her mind was drifting off to some interesting places when she could put Rory in the same sentence as the words *serial killer*.

"Yes, ma'am," Rory responded. He put his hand out in front of him and stepped aside so Emerson could follow Polly first.

"Booth or table?" Polly asked.

"I'm not picky," Emerson responded.

The café seating looked comfortable. In the middle of the dining room was a row of booths. There were tables sprinkled on each side. Polly took them to a booth smack in the middle of the place. Emerson took a seat, realizing she'd just put her back to the door. The idea that she now had to watch behind her everywhere she went gave her a creepy feeling she couldn't ignore.

"Menus are on the table," Polly said. "I'll be right back. I better let Manne know we aren't spreading the word of your return."

She disappeared for less than a minute while Emerson got the lay of the land after being handed an illuminated menu. The paper was so old, it had turned yellow despite the protective covering. At eight thirty in the evening, activity was almost at a dead stop. A young couple looked to be finishing up their meal at a table in the corner. She assumed they were on a date with the way they leaned across the table and seemed to hang on each other's every word. Emerson tried to remember the last time she was on a date as interesting as theirs seemed to be. How sad was that? Her thirtieth birthday had come and gone, and her dating life had come to a screeching halt.

There were worse things, she thought. Like finding out the father she knew and loved had lied to her for all of those thirty years. Losing her only parent had been hard enough without the betrayal. She kept looping back to one question. Why?

Polly returned a moment later and set two waters down. "Have you decided what you want?"

"Chicken-fried steak, corn on the cob and fried okra," Emerson said. It was a shame she hadn't had fried food since the fair. October was her favorite month in North Texas for its cooler temperatures and the event that brought pig races, livestock and rides all together in one venue.

"What about to drink? Or are you good with water?" Polly asked.

"Tea," Emerson said.

"Sweet or unsweet?"

"Can I do half and half?" Regular tea was too bitter and sweet tea too much.

"Sure thing," Polly said with a wide smile before looking to Rory. "How about you?"

"Same," he said, placing the menu back in the sleeve. "Except coffee instead of tea."

"I'll have these out in a minute," Polly said as she beamed at Rory. "It sure is good to have you home."

"Just visiting," he quickly corrected. "And it sure is good to see you."

Polly disappeared into the kitchen through a set of stainless-steel double doors with a pair of windows that looked like cruise ship portals. The doors were marked In and Out. The signs might not have been fancy, but they got the job done.

"How long have you known Polly?" she asked Rory after he finished checking his cell phone and responding to texts.

His cell dinged again almost the instant he dropped it inside his shirt pocket. He flashed eyes at Emerson. "My apologies. I need to respond to this."

"Of course," she said, not wanting to stand in between him and his work. A thought occurred to her that the texts could be coming in from someone other than an employee or client. After he finished the communication, she should probably ask whether or not he was single. She wouldn't come right out with the question. There were other ways of asking without carrying a banner.

Head down, he didn't look up again until Polly arrived with heaping plates of food.

"I won't go hungry eating here," Emerson said. "And it smells delicious."

"Wasn't sure about gravy, so I put it in a ramekin on the side there." Polly motioned. She glanced around the table before placing her hands on her hips. "Ketchup is already on the table if you need it. What else can I get you?"

Rory finally looked up and immediately shifted his gaze to Emerson. A zing of attraction sizzled from across the table.

"I have everything I need right here," she said, picking up the napkin-rolled silverware. "I can't wait to dig in."

RORY'S CELL PHONE dinged almost the minute he picked up his fork. He flashed a look of apology toward Emerson before retrieving it again. He answered Liv's text and then sent another one asking her not to text for the next fifteen minutes unless she was bleeding or on fire. He could almost hear her rolling her eyes as she read it. Her response came in the form of a thumbs-up to his message, and he was grateful that had been the finger she'd chosen.

"Sorry about that," he said to Emerson after tucking his cell inside his shirt pocket. He couldn't help but quirk a smile at the thought of Liv doing anything that could get her into trouble with him. He'd been a strict father, spoiling her with love instead monetary gifts. So far, she seemed to be turning out great. And yet, he couldn't help but wonder when the other shoe was going to drop. He was just thankful she hadn't figured out how little he knew what he was doing when it came to parenting. He'd gotten better with practice, he hoped. At the very least, he'd become more confident in his decisions.

Fortunately, the gods smiled on him when they gave him Liv because she was a good student and a solid soccer player. She surrounded herself with nice friends who seemed to have her back. It was the best he could hope for, eye-rolling aside.

"Family?" she asked.

"Yes," he confirmed. He knew she meant family in Cider Creek, and he wasn't exactly lying when he confirmed her guess. So, why did he feel like a jerk for not explaining the messages and calls earlier had been from his daughter?

"Wife?" Emerson asked, catching him off guard.

"No, nothing like that," he said, shaking his head for emphasis, unsure why he felt the need to be so emphatic. He liked Emerson. She was in need of a friend, especially someone who could help her navigate Cider Creek. A tiny voice in the back of his mind picked that moment to point out the fact he didn't know the town any longer. One of his buddies would do a better job of helping her figure out town politics, who to avoid and who might be of help.

After his encounter with Bynum Ross, Rory realized he no longer knew who he could trust.

"Oh," Emerson said. "I just thought with the phone calls and the texts that…" She put a hand up.

"It's none of my business and I appreciate your help. Please, don't feel like you have to explain anything to me."

"No, it's fine." He suddenly realized how all this must look to an outsider. He wished he could come clean about having a child. It would make this conversation go a whole lot smoother. It wasn't right for Emerson to know before his own mother. It occurred to him that Theo had brought up Leah. Was that why Emerson suddenly had questions about his relationship status? It was only logical she would want to know who was helping her. "I was in a relationship a long time ago. It didn't work out, so there isn't much to say there."

"She was important to you, though," Emerson said after looking into his eyes.

"At one time, yes," he said.

"The ship has sailed?" she asked in between bites.

"In a manner of speaking," he confirmed. The fact Leah hadn't been back to Cider Creek in all these years surprised him even though the only family she had left in town was her grandmother. Her mother had raised Leah on her own, then relocated to Houston right before graduation to move in with her boyfriend. Throughout school, Leah had talked about how hard being a single mother was on her mother. Mrs. Grove had moved in with her mother when Leah was a baby. With all the complaining Leah had done over the years about her mother having to sacrifice her life, he was even more surprised that Leah could abandon her infant daughter.

Had she been afraid history would repeat itself? That he would eventually grow tired of coming home every night when his friends were out having a good time? That he would do what Leah's father had done and disappear?

Rory couldn't count the number of times Leah had condemned her father for walking out on the family. Her leaving was a cat's-in-the-cradle moment if ever there'd been one. There were times when she would slip into sadness so deep all Rory could do was wait it out with her. Certain things would trigger her and send her in a downward spiral. Things like daddy-daughter dances would send her into a funk. She'd cry on his shoulder.

He could live a thousand lives and still wouldn't understand some folks.

"I'm not trying to get into your personal business," Emerson said after clearing her throat. He realized he'd lost track of time in his reverie. "Just make conversation."

"Sorry," he said. "You're not." He heaved a sigh and thought long and hard about how much he wanted to share about his relationship with Leah. A few bits of information couldn't hurt. "Everyone in town believed that my high school sweetheart and I were going to get married and I reckon they'll be surprised just like Theo and Jimmy that Leah and I broke up. We moved away together after graduation and, though

I've lost track of her, doesn't seem like either of us came back, which isn't a huge surprise on her part considering her mother moved away and she didn't get along with her grandmother."

Her eyebrow shot up, but she kept quiet. This seemed like a good time to turn the tables.

"You? Is there a husband or serious boyfriend waiting back in Arlington?" he asked.

"Oh, uh, no," she stammered. "Not even close. Did you see that couple over there in the corner when we first walked in?"

He nodded. They'd been loved up, so he didn't stare.

"I can't remember the last time I had a date that looked as good as theirs did," she admitted before her cheeks flushed. "I've dated. Don't get me wrong. But no one has ever enticed me to lean over a table and gaze into their eyes."

"Believe me," he started, "I understand. Besides, I wouldn't have time for anyone to be more important than my..." He stopped in time to substitute *daughter* with, "work."

Based on the way she was studying him right now, she wasn't buying it.

"Building a business from the ground up requires a whole lot of time and attention," he explained. "The business becomes like your family and the thought of handing it off to someone else, even for a little bit, becomes akin to turning over your firstborn."

"Once you've put your blood, sweat and tears into

a place, I can imagine how difficult it would be to let go." She folded her hands together and set them on the edge of the table. "I can't say that I've had anything in my life that compares."

"What about relationships? Someone as intelligent and beautiful as you are must have had a few," he said.

"If you're asking whether or not I've been in love with someone, I'd have to say not for a long time. What I thought was love turned out to be something else," she said. "My father was overprotective of me when I was younger, so dating was out of the question."

"If I had a daughter, she wouldn't date until her thirties," he quipped, only half joking. He was pretty certain every father of a teenage daughter had the same thought about buying a shotgun if he didn't own one already and cleaning it in the living room if she brought a date home.

Emerson's laugh was short-lived. "The idea must be implanted into fathers then. Mine wasn't too far off."

"Sounds like he loved you and was trying to do the right thing by you," he said when she sighed.

"I mean, yes," she said. "Except how else was I supposed to learn about dating if I didn't start doing it until I was eighteen?"

"Eighteen?" He didn't hide his shock. "Seriously?"

"Not so much as a peck on the cheek until I'd graduated high school," she said. "Made the learning curve steep and the mistakes bigger."

Rory couldn't help but wonder how much of the secret identity of her mother played a role in the actions of Emerson's father, or if she was out of danger with that truck camped outside.

Chapter Seven

Emerson didn't normally spill her guts to a person she'd only known for a matter of hours. She chalked it up to the stress of the day, the loneliness she'd recently felt and the fact Rory was easy to talk to.

"If you ever have a daughter, do everyone a favor and don't keep her locked in an ivory tower," she said after finishing the last bite of the best chicken-fried steak she'd ever tasted.

"I'll keep that in mind," he said as an emotion passed behind his eyes that she had trouble nailing down. He was hiding something, and Emerson hated secrets. Of course, there was no reason for her to dig around in Rory's past. The simple fact he was looking out for her when she needed a friend was all she needed to know about the man. The few folks she'd met so far seemed to hold him in high regard. He was decent and kind. So what if he had an 'it's-complicated' relationship lurking somewhere in the background. He didn't seem to want to share.

"Believe me, I can give you a whole lot of advice

about having a daughter when the day comes," she continued as Polly joined them.

"Did either of you save room for dessert?" she asked, looking proud of the fact they'd both cleaned their plates.

"As tempting as that sounds, I don't think I could stuff another bite in my mouth," Emerson said.

"I'm all good here." Rory patted a stomach that most likely was nothing but washboard abs underneath his casual button-down shirt. But his stomach muscles weren't her business, either. "I'll take the check." He glanced over at Emerson as though looking for approval that it was okay if he picked up the tab.

"As much as you've done for me today, it should be the other way around," Emerson stated. "But I'm not offended by the offer." She needed to figure out a way to pay him back or just show her gratitude for everything he'd done for her. He'd said he would be visiting his family home for a few days, so maybe she could send over one of the pies on Polly's menu as a thank-you gift.

"No bill tonight," Polly said emphatically. "Rory Hayes coming home is a celebration."

"It's just a visit," he clarified. "No need to organize a parade."

Polly cracked a wide smile.

"Either way, your meals are on the house," she said. "Next time, I'll let you pay *and* I hope you won't skip dessert." She winked. If adorable had a face, it would be Polly's. She had the whole spunky-and-kind grandmotherly thing down pat.

"Thank you," Emerson stated. "I'll be sure to stop by tomorrow since I'm staying at the inn down the street, and I have no idea how long it'll be before my Bronco is up and running again."

"We open at 6:00 a.m.," Polly informed. "And no one can beat our skillets."

Rory nodded. "You still have those on the menu?"

"Sure do," Polly said. "You should stop by too."

"I might do just that," he stated. "Besides, it's too late to head to the ranch tonight. I'll most likely grab a room in town."

Emerson's stomach performed a little flip at the thought of Rory sleeping in the same B&B. Thinking too much about the handsome rancher turned successful business owner wasn't a good idea while she was so tired, and he'd literally saved her backside today. From stepping in to defend her to Bynum Ross to being there moments after the truck had tried to run her off the road, sheer luck had him in the right place at the right time. Rory was two for two in the random-luck department. She could only hope it would hold.

"Ready?" Rory asked.

She nodded, once again thanked Polly for the meal and then stood up. After Rory said his good-bye, they walked out the door together. She immediately glanced over to see if the truck was gone now that the cute couple had left. There it sat in the dark.

Maybe she was reading too much into it. After the day she'd had, there was no wonder she was looking for ghosts to pop out from behind a tree. As they walked toward his pickup, motion to her right caused her to practically jump out of her skin. Without debating her actions, she immediately grabbed Rory's arm, digging her fingers into flesh in a death grip.

All he did in response was chuckle and pull her closer to him. There was so much heat and chemistry pinging between them, she wouldn't need a jacket despite the cooler night temperatures.

"Cat," he said, motioning toward the black cat with amber-colored eyes.

"Meow," the kitty responded in a tone that suggested he or she was offended.

Now it was Emerson's turn to laugh. It probably came out sounding like nervous laughter, but she would take what she could get.

"No hurry, but I think you might be drawing blood, so if you wanted to let go it would be much appreciated," he said gently and with just enough humor that she didn't feel completely awful.

"Right." She immediately did just that, withdrawing her hand. "It's been a day."

"Yes, it has," he said. "One I hope isn't repeated tomorrow or the next day."

"Same here." Emerson released a long, slow sigh. "This has been the most terrifying day of my life in some ways." She buckled up before he made the short drive to the B&B. "In others, it has been satisfying in a strange way."

"How so?" His eyebrow shot up.

"I've lived a pretty sheltered life and had no idea my father was keeping secrets," she began. "Looking back, I probably should have realized something was going on. There were only a couple of pictures of my 'mother' around." She made air quotes around the word *mother*. "I didn't have a connection to the woman in the pictures and I always thought there had to be something wrong with me. I tried my best to force one but it didn't work."

"You must have noticed the two of you didn't look that much alike," Rory pointed out and it was true.

"There were similarities, but that was my first thought when I overheard my aunt. I kept thinking that I should step into the room and argue with her, except that it resonated with me," she admitted. "I just kept thinking it might be true and thought back to the photos that I had no connection with. For years, I convinced myself the reason I didn't connect with the woman in the photos was because I didn't remember her. Now, I realize there was more to it."

"My family has a long history," he said after a thoughtful pause. "We go way back and have been tied to my grandfather's ranching business so much that it was our identity throughout our growing years. I can't imagine what it would be like to find out it was a lie." He turned toward her after parking in the lot at the B&B. "Not knowing where you came from or who you are must be the worst kind of hurt. One of your parents lying to you about your identity…" He paused for a few beats. "I have to think there was a good reason behind the deception."

"Thank you," she said, appreciating the honesty in his voice. There was a rawness to it that soothed her. "After Bynum Ross's reaction to me showing up with the picture, I'm left wondering if there was a darker reason and I'm not leaving until I get to the bottom of it."

She was determined to find the truth. Maybe it was the grief talking and the fact she couldn't seem to have a good cry. Going back to Arlington without answers wasn't an option because she doubted that she would be able to sleep again. The only way to be able to put this behind her and move on was to face it. Doing so alone scared her after today's events.

"You mentioned that you're staying at the B&B as well," Emerson said, figuring she might as well go for broke while she had his attention.

"That's right," Rory said. He was about to offer to stay next door if she would feel more comfortable.

"Have you stayed in a room here before?" she asked.

"I've visited."

"Are there any connected rooms?" she continued.

"We can ask. I'm happy to sleep on the floor in your room if it would make you feel better," he said, thinking the sacrifice on his part would be worth it if Emerson could relax and get a good night of sleep.

Her mind had to be spinning out over the day's events and he could close his eyes and conk out under pretty much any circumstances. He'd annoyed women in his rare past relationships for his ability to stay awake nineteen hours a day, needing only five hours to recharge. He'd been told just how annoying he was by those who worked for him as well, especially when he sent an email at midnight and was back up by five ready and able to respond.

"Your back would be a nightmare tomorrow if you took the hard floor." Emerson shook her head. "Can't allow it." She paused and turned to look at him. Their eyes met and a small fireworks show went off inside his rib cage. "We can work something else out."

Rather than sit there until his chest caught fire, he nodded then exited the truck. He came around the front of the vehicle to her side before opening the door. The thought of sleeping in the same room overnight with Emerson stirred a place in his chest that had been dormant since Leah.

He made a phone call, apologizing for the late notice.

"Come on inside," Doris Randolph said after she opened the front door. "If I'd known you were coming, I would have kept everything unlocked."

"I hope this is no trouble," Rory said. The truck from earlier drove off in the opposite direction, so he wasn't able to get a plate number.

"None at all," Doris said. She was tall, thin and

always wore her gray hair piled on top of her head. She had the body of a ballet dancer with long and lean lines. She may have mentioned something about dance inspirations when Rory was young. He was just now realizing how much Doris could have taught him all those years ago.

"How many rooms?" Doris asked, walking behind the counter before opening a drawer.

"One," he said after making introductions.

Questions danced in Doris's eyes, but she clamped her mouth shut.

"Has there been trouble in town lately involving teenagers and trucks?" he asked, figuring it couldn't hurt to inquire.

Doris's eyebrow shot up.

"None that I know of," she said.

Emerson had been quiet up to now other than introducing herself. She reached inside her handbag and produced the photo from this afternoon.

"I'm trying to track down a relative." She set the picture down on the counter and angled it toward Doris. "Does this woman look familiar?"

Doris squinted before reaching for a pair of reading glasses. Her face scrunched up as she homed in on the woman holding the baby. Her expression dropped. "No. Sorry. Can't help you."

She couldn't get a key in Rory's hand fast enough.

"It's too late for turndown service. Waffles are at six sharp." Doris looked up at Rory. A helpless look crossed her features. "Off you go to room seven."

Chapter Eight

Emerson realized pretty darn fast she and Rory had just been dismissed. Without hesitation, she followed Rory up the staircase and down the hallway to the room at the end. Seven was her lucky number and, the way she figured it, she was overdue for some good luck on this trip. Unless she counted Rory, of course. There, she had no idea how she'd fallen into such good fortune.

"Did you see the look on her face when she saw the picture?" she asked Rory.

"She knows something," he stated after closing and locking their door.

"What could be so bad about her that makes everyone shut down the minute they see her photo and deny knowing she existed?" she asked.

"They might be protecting her identity," he reasoned after a pause.

"Think someone will show up in the middle of the night to…?"

She stopped herself right there. Giving in to fear

or expecting the worst never helped make a bad situation better.

Rory slid an armchair over to the door and wedged it against the handle. "That should stop anyone from coming through that door. Or slow them down at the very least. Either way, it'll give me time to react."

A shiver ran down her spine. This was real. She was in danger. Or at the very least, someone was trying to send her a message or make her go away.

"What if this is all a scare tactic?" she asked. There was still a glimmer of hope no one wanted to do actual harm to her.

"I can't take the risk when it comes to your safety," Rory said as he moved to the window and checked the locks. He opened a couple of drawers then closed them, looking dissatisfied. He moved to the closet and pulled out the luggage holder, sizing it up.

Knowing Rory had her back meant the world to her. Growing up, she'd spent weekends practically under lock and key. While her friends were at sleepovers, she watched movies and read books. Thankfully, internet and gaming provided a small connection to the outside world. But online friendships through a game, while nice, weren't the same as making memories at sleepovers like her friends did. It caused most of her relationships to fall under the on-the-surface type. She'd been allowed to work at a craft store, which pretty much killed any possibility of meeting guys her age.

"I'd like to secure the window better, but there

isn't anything here I can use," he said on a frustrated-sounding sigh. "At least we're on the second floor. That's a small help, but I'll take what I can get at this point."

The seriousness of his expression worried her more than anything. It meant he was as concerned as she was the driver of the first truck had meant to harm her and the second truck had been sent to pinpoint her location. She bet he'd expected her to be alone tonight.

"Maybe we can place something on top of there that will make a noise if it drops, like the alarm clock. It might be thin enough to stay put," she said as she bent down and then unplugged the alarm. The front was flat and she hoped it would balance on the thick windowsill.

Rory was already nodding his head. "It could work."

"Let's hope." Emerson balanced the alarm clock facedown on the sill. She peered out the window, but it was too dark to see anything. The view to and from this window was camouflaged by trees.

The idea worked. She turned around, proud as punch. Rory stood behind her. She must have taken a step back with the half twirl because she was face-to-chest with the man. And oh what a chest it was. Even through the cotton of his shirt there were muscles for days.

This close, his spicy aftershave filled her senses. Emerson brought her hand up to brace herself against the onslaught but touching him only made her attraction ten times worse. An electrical impulse shot through her. Her brain seemed to disengage when she was this close because instead of bracing herself, her fingers roamed.

He brought his hand up to clasp hers and for a split second, she expected him to tell her this was a bad idea. The moment quickly faded when he lowered his head against her forehead. She could inhale his breath. The smell of coffee on his lips tempted her to taste the dark roast blend.

Rather than debate her next actions, she did exactly what she wanted…kissed him. The kiss was so tender she nearly melted. She could stand there and kiss Rory Hayes for days. Exhaustion was kicking in and the stress of the day was catching up to her. She pulled back first.

"I'm sorry," she immediately said, bringing the back of her hand up to her mouth.

"I'm not," he quickly countered with a look in his eyes that reassured her that he was telling the truth. It wasn't helping with her impulse control.

"It shouldn't happen again," she said without a whole lot of enthusiasm. It couldn't, which accounted for the lack of commitment on her part. Desire had nothing to do with the decision.

"I think we both know that," he said with a small smile. "Plus, we need sleep."

Nice of him to pretend he'd been the one to yawn

three times on the short ride over. "A shower would be wonderful. Is it asking too much?"

"There's a shared bathroom two doors down," he said. "I can stand outside the door and wait until you're finished just to be on the safe side."

She probably didn't want to ask how he knew the layout of the rooms up here so well.

"I used to do handyman work for Ms. Doris way back when if she was in between help," he stated. "My mother knows pretty much everyone in town and sent her boys to help when someone was in need. Never bothered me much to do it. Plus, I always got paid in baked goods, so it was a good deal from my end."

"Got it," she said with a salute.

"We need to rest," he said. "Let me show you to the bathroom. There are always extra supplies in the cabinet, by the way. Doris likes to be stocked in case a guest forgets something. Plus, there are robes folded up. Actually, there's probably a fresh one hanging over the door if memory serves and Doris hasn't changed." He took a look around the sweet room that still had rose-print wallpaper and a matching duvet, and cracked a smile. "From the looks of this place, nothing has."

"It's probably a good thing then," she said. "Because I wouldn't mind freshening up and in the shock of the accident, I forgot to grab my overnight bag from the Bronco."

"We can swing by and pick it up first thing in the morning," he said.

Maybe they could get Doris talking in the morning as well.

RORY FORCED HIS thoughts away from the fact Emerson was stripped naked on the other side of the bathroom door as he stood in the hallway, playing bodyguard. He didn't mind the role considering she needed one, but his lips still sizzled from the kiss and blood flew south every time he thought about it.

Mentally chastising himself, he refocused attention on planning their next steps. If they made it through the night without any interruptions, he intended to ask Doris what the face was about. It seemed some of the older folks in Cider Creek knew something about the woman in the photo, and the few people they'd asked had blown them off. Rory thought about his own family secrets. Speaking of which, it was late but he needed to check in with Liv. Being back in Cider Creek made him come face-to-face with the reality he'd been living a lie by keeping her a secret. No one in town knew he had a child and she was twelve years old.

He let that sink in for a moment as he fished his cell phone out of his pocket and checked the screen. Liv's smiling face greeted him as his screen saver, filling the screen as much as his heart as she often did.

No matter how awful a day had been, seeing his

daughter's smile made everything else seem small by comparison. Liv had a way of making Rory see what was truly important in life even when the day seemed stacked against him.

She also had a way of blowing up his phone with texts now that she'd been given her own. He cursed the fact he must have turned the volume off his cell. There were half a dozen messages here. Thankfully, no calls. He would be worried if she'd been trying to reach him for something important. His daughter was in good hands and a growing piece of him was eager for her to meet her extended family. Despite having a grandfather who was stubborn as a mule and grumpy as a starved bear, Rory's memories were filled with good times growing up at the ranch with his brothers and sisters.

Looking back now, he felt more than a twinge of guilt for allowing his grandfather to dictate Liv's relationship with her grandmother. Or should he say nonrelationship? It had become so easy to stay away. His life was in North Texas. His business was thriving after years of keeping his head down and working. His daughter was in a good place too, when he really thought about it. Would learning about a family he'd kept from her all these years damage their relationship?

Rory hadn't given himself a chance to consider how unfair the situation might have been to Liv. Granted, in the early years, he'd done a whole lot of feeling sorry for Liv and, as much as he didn't like to admit it, himself. He'd licked his wounds and tended to his bruised ego for longer than he probably should have after Leah took off. There was a whole lot of self-pity happening in between diaper changes. Then, he'd bucked up and promised to put the past behind him. Had he lumped Cider Creek into the same category as Leah? Coming back without her after how his grandfather had behaved had been a hit his ego couldn't take. Plus, he refused to take his daughter where she wasn't wanted. If Duncan Hayes didn't see Liv as a gift to this world, Rory hadn't wanted to take her to the man's ranch. In Rory's mind, Duncan didn't deserve to know Liv.

Then there was the home and community he'd set up in Mesquite. He checked the phone. Liv sent a picture of a hairless cat. Again. Her obsession with them was to the point of funny. Her reasoning for wanting one was even funnier: she wanted to put sweaters on it—apparently, a hairless cat is cold most of the time—and she wanted to name the cat Dobby. Yes, from the megapopular, worldwide phenomenon about a certain boy wizard.

Rory wanted to give that girl the world, but she'd head off to college in six years, and he'd be stuck with Dobby. Didn't seem like a fair trade to him.

Still, Liv made Rory smile with the request and the photos. There was something very comforting about knowing exactly how her mind worked. He realized that wouldn't last long as it was already beginning to slip away. The eye rolls were only part of the problem. In all honesty, Liv had been pushing him away recently and he wondered how much of it was his fault and how much of it was nature's. She was getting to the age where she could use female advice, and it terrified him.

He responded to her multiple texts with one. Basically, it said no to the cat and to go to bed. He chuckled at the same time the bathroom door opened behind him.

"Hey," Emerson said.

It took a second to realize he was blocking the door before he stepped aside to allow passage.

"You're welcome to go into the next room or wait inside while I brush my teeth and grab a shower," he said. It wasn't lost on him that she was wearing nothing but a towel. Her clothes were a folded bundle in her hands.

"Okay," she said before clearing her throat. They needed to push past the attraction if they were going to get any sleep tonight. Plus, he hadn't felt anything like this in far too long. His brain half decided it was the circumstances and not the woman. He'd always been the one to step in when someone was being bullied. Cider Creek wasn't exactly showing Emerson a warm welcome.

He quickly tucked his cell back inside his jeans pocket.

"How should we do this?" she asked, tightening the towel.

"I'll leave the bathroom door unlocked in case you get scared," he said.

"I'm pretty certain that I already said this, but thank you," Emerson said as she slipped underneath the covers. "I trust you with my life, so please feel free to sleep on the bed."

He glanced at the sheets and, for a split second, worried if it was a good idea to climb inside. He disappeared into the bathroom for a quick shower, once again leaving the door unlocked. When he returned, he decided to sleep on top of the covers. Besides, he was fully clothed. There wasn't a whole lot of temptation in that.

Rory moved to the left side of the bed. With his large frame, she was thankful it was a king. He stretched his legs and leaned his head back on the pillow as Emerson turned to her side, her back to him.

Her clean citrus scent washed over him. Rory cracked a smile. Normally, he was full of self-control, but his supply wasn't as plentiful tonight. Not that he'd try anything. He'd never force himself on a woman. But considering he'd turned down more dates in the past couple of years than he could count, he wouldn't turn her away if she propositioned him. Plus, figuring out how to fill up an entire evening with conversation wasn't his forte. He came home from work tired, not ready to force conversation with someone he barely knew. When he thought about his life in Mesquite in those terms, it seemed lonely. It wasn't. He had Liv and she filled the entire house with conversation.

Except that she was getting older now and wanted to talk to her friends more than she wanted to spend Friday nights with him. He'd miss those times when she wanted nothing more than a bucket of microwave popcorn and some type of sour candy as they watched a movie together. He'd had his fill of cartoons, but he'd managed to find a few to watch with his little girl that weren't complete torture.

Liv would like Emerson. The two were equally independent. He wanted to get Emerson's opinion on what he should be telling Liv about her mother. After watching the torment in Emerson's eyes, he knew he had to do everything within his power to protect Liv from an even bigger heartache. Even if it meant tracking Leah down and introducing her to her child. And he needed to come clean about the rest of the family too.

There was a whole lot of reckoning that needed to happen in his life. Liv's world was about to be turned upside down. It was time to face the music.

Chapter Nine

Emerson woke to an empty bed. She startled at the realization that she was alone. An equally forceful calm came over her the second she saw Rory, shirtless, sitting in the chair that had been wedged against the door. Head down and legs crossed at the ankles, his cell phone balanced on his thigh.

She couldn't help but wonder who he was conversing with. More than once, he'd quickly tucked his cell inside his pocket whenever she walked toward him. He'd said he wasn't in a relationship and yet the signs were there. Why would he lie about it?

Her movement caused him to stir. After scanning the room, he rubbed his eyes. When he sat forward, he rested his elbows on his knees.

"Morning," she said after taking a deep breath.

"How did you sleep?" he asked. His voice had a gruff early-morning timbre that threatened to pierce her armor, but no matter how long it'd been since she'd had a decent date, a man with secrets wasn't and would never be right for her.

"Good," she answered. "How about you?"

"I got a couple hours," he admitted. His cell phone lit up and she was almost certain there was a picture of a female on his lock screen. Perfect timing, she decided. There was an easy and charming way about Rory Hayes that made it easy to lower her guard when she was around him. The kiss they'd shared, even though it wasn't much more than a peck, caused her lips to tingle even thinking about it.

"Excuse me," Rory said. "I need to take this."

"Be my guest," she said, a little surprised when he stood up and stepped into the hallway. She glanced around. The first thing she noticed was the small pile of neatly stacked clothing on the dresser. How on earth did Rory manage to have her clothes cleaned? She figured she had time to change while he made the phone call to some important female in his life. Who that could be was a mystery.

While Rory was out of the room, she quickly changed back into her clothes. His voice was a low hum from the hallway. One she couldn't allow to get inside her since it had a way of making her want to forget that he was keeping secrets.

The door opened and she immediately glanced down to make certain all her clothes were on. When she looked up, the blood drained from her face.

"What's wrong?" she asked.

"Do you remember Jimmy from yesterday?" he asked.

"Yes. Why?"

"He just called and asked us to come down to the shop as soon as possible," Rory said. "His shop was broken into and so was your Bronco."

Anger boiled to the surface, bubbling over before she could get a handle on it.

"What would anyone want with my...?"

It dawned on her.

"Someone wants to know exactly who I am, don't they?" she asked, but it was more statement than question.

"That would be my guess," he admitted. He checked her out. "Good. I'm glad you found the clothes Doris washed for you this morning."

"What time did that happen, by the way?" she asked.

"Around 4:00 a.m.," he said as he located his T-shirt and then shrugged it on over broad shoulders. He threw on his button down next, tucked his cell phone in his front pocket, and said, "Doris has waffles waiting downstairs. She heard me on the phone and called up from the bottom of the stairs."

Doris must have a quiet voice because Emerson sure didn't hear anything besides his.

"I'm ready to go as soon as I make a pit stop in the bathroom," she said, needing to brush her teeth. Morning breath was always the worst. As for makeup, she probably looked like a disaster and didn't concern herself with putting on anything other than eyeliner and concealer, unless she was going on a date. It wasn't lost on her that she was already searching for lip gloss in her purse. She turned to Rory as she walked by. "Is anything missing from my Bronco?"

"I think that's why he wants you to come down," he said. "I asked about your overnight bag, and he said he didn't recall seeing one."

"Well, isn't that just great?" she said under her breath as she exited the room. She would ask if the day could get any worse but was afraid of the answer. She also realized all of this would be near-impossible without Rory's help.

Not five minutes later, she exited the bathroom to a waiting Rory. He bopped inside next and it took him all of three minutes to be ready to go. She waited as the smell of waffles caused her stomach to growl. It smelled beyond amazing but all she really wanted was a cup of coffee. Her nerves were fried and it wasn't even eight o'clock yet. How was that for a start to the day? What did she even have inside Bronc other than her overnight bag? A box of tissue was always in the back seat. There was probably spare change in the console and possibly the glove box. She couldn't remember the last time she looked in there. She'd heard the newer, fancier models had an in-console safe but hers most definitely did not.

Emerson followed Rory downstairs and into the kitchen, where Doris was standing at the sink humming. He cleared his throat.

"Oh, hey there," Doris said as she spun around with a dish in hand.

"We have to go," Rory said after a smile and a wink. "There's been a situation at Jimmy's shop involving Emerson's vehicle."

"Is that right?" Doris asked, but the question was rhetorical. Was there something in her eyes that said she expected something like this?

"I REALIZE I'VE been away from town far too long," Rory began. "But since when did we start treating strangers this way?"

A half dozen emotions crossed Doris's features before she finally spoke up.

"I'm sorry folks aren't as friendly as they used to be," she said in a voice that was more like a warning. "There are people in Cider Creek who don't want to bring up the past is all I can say." She shrugged. "Now, I have coffee in to-go mugs. There are waffles." She locked gazes with Rory. "It's all I can do right now." There was a hint of apology in her eyes. "I wish there was more. Believe me."

Rory made a mental note to circle back and maybe come at this from a different angle. He didn't want to make anyone uncomfortable or put anyone else in harm's way, but this was serious and getting more so by the hour.

"Understood," was all he said for now. "And I appreciate everything you've done for us this morning." He also realized she might be taking a risk in having them stay the night. His cell buzzed as he took the offering of coffee and waffles. He set them down and then checked his screen. As he glanced up at Emerson, he felt the cold chill from a little while ago return. The air had changed between the sizzling kiss and now. This wasn't the time to figure it out. There were a whole lot of thoughts rolling through his mind, none that he needed to focus on while he was trying to sort through why the town seemed to have lost its collective mind recently. The only thing he could think of was that Emerson had stirred up a hornet's nest. She didn't deserve any of this, which made him even more curious about the story behind the woman in the picture.

"Thank you, Rory," Doris said sincerely. He got the impression she was between a rock and a hard place. He didn't like what was transpiring one bit, but there was more than one way to get to the truth.

He nodded before accepting her offerings. The two of them walked to his vehicle, hands loaded up. He set the foil-wrapped waffle on top of his hood before reaching into his pocket for the key fob. A tap on the button unlocked the door. Emerson started looking for a place to set her food down.

"I got this," he said, opening the door for her.

Her thank-you sounded obligatory and was missing all the warmth from the other times she'd said the same words. He noted the change in temperature between them as odd and moved on. As he claimed the driver's seat, his cell phone went off. He checked the screen, keeping it tilted toward him so he was the only one who could see the screen. It didn't seem to matter. Emerson kept her gaze forward as she downed a waffle. He cut her some slack considering the day wasn't exactly off to a good start and tried not to let the chill bother him.

The message from Liv was telling him that she was heading off to school. Since he normally went into work at about the time she was waking up for school, he didn't pass by her in the mornings. She'd been fully capable of getting herself up and ready since third grade so he didn't worry about her. She walked to school with the neighbor's kid. If anything went south, Maddie's mom was right there. Plus, he'd moved to the safest neighborhood he could find in his price range at the time. Now, he could move them up to something even bigger but he'd learned a long time ago that higher cost didn't necessarily mean better. Liv was happy where they were. She liked her friends. There were moms in the neighborhood who always looked out for her. Good mothers amazed him in that way. They didn't stop with their own children. The really good ones cared about all the kids. The stark contrast to Leah, who'd cared only about herself, wasn't lost on him.

He guessed some women were motherhood material and some weren't. Same went for fathers. The trick seemed to be that some didn't seem to find out which way they landed until they were actually holding their first child.

Tucking his cell phone away, he started the engine and backed out of the parking spot. He glanced around for signs of the truck from last night or the one from yesterday, but neither was in sight.

The ride over was quiet and he managed to get down most of the cup of coffee before arriving at Jimmy's. As soon as he parked, Emerson exited the vehicle, to-go cup firmly in her grip. Since she was perfectly capable of opening her own doors, he didn't say anything when she walked inside Jimmy's first. Opening doors was a courtesy that had been ingrained in him as a show of respect, but the option was always in a woman's court. Clearly, she was no longer interested in his chivalry.

Jimmy's place was the same as when his father owned it, with new chairs in the small boxed-in waiting room. The coffee table was newer but still managed to look like it came from a garage sale. The top half of the wall between the lobby and the work bay was all window.

Rory had noticed right away the small punch hole through the glass of the front door. The jagged pieces of glass crunched as he walked inside.

"Ms.—"

"Call me Emerson," she said, all business in her tone. "Please."

Theo nodded as Jimmy walked over to Rory. The two shook hands.

"I don't know what happened here," Jimmy said with a look of frustration and…loss. "In all the years I've been running the place, nothing like this has ever happened." Jimmy raked his fingers through his hair.

"We know Emerson's overnight bag is missing. I'm wondering what else is gone," Rory stated, not liking where any of this was going. Did the person responsible believe she might have left the picture inside the Bronco? She'd kept it inside her purse so far. He remembered the way she'd tucked it back inside at B-T yesterday. "There wasn't anything important inside my bag, just a few outfits and toiletries."

Theo was walking Emerson into the bay area, warning her to be careful. Rory followed a few steps behind as Jimmy brought up the rear.

"When my wife and I dated, she kept her vehicle spotlessly clean," Theo said. "Nothing was ever out of place, but she didn't keep much inside like I do. She had a yoga mat rolled up in the back seat and a couple of blocks for when she took class. That was about it."

"I don't even keep a yoga mat inside the Bronco," Emerson said before clearing her throat. From behind, he couldn't get a good read on her face. Based on her voice, though, she was crushed. "All I should have had in there was a box of tissues in the back, my overnight bag and whatever was inside the console. Mostly change and breath mints."

Theo nodded before walking over to the glove box.

"I dusted for prints, but it would be good for you to confirm the contents are still there," he said. "Most folks keep their vehicle's manual, repair records and insurance information inside," he pointed out.

Emerson walked over to the passenger side before opening the door and then the glove box. She stood there, staring, and he could tell in an instant that something was wrong.

"What is it?" he asked, coming around the front of the vehicle to look at whatever she found inside.

"I always toss my insurance card on top of the owner's manual," she said. He did the same, so he instantly understood what she was alluding to. She lifted the book and, sure enough, the card was underneath.

"Someone took these out and then tossed the card back inside first," he said.

"That's my guess because it's always here when I have to replace it every year." She set the owner's manual on top of the passenger seat. "Why would they do that?" The reason seemed to dawn on her as she asked the question. "My home address."

Rory looked to Theo, who nodded.

"That's right," Theo confirmed.

Emerson shivered.

"They know where I live."

Chapter Ten

"I need to get back to Arlington to see what they're after." At this point, Emerson's blood boiled.

"I'll make a call to Arlington PD and let them know trouble might be on the way," Theo said. "May I see that card?"

"Yes, of course." Emerson handed it over before glancing over at Rory.

Phone in hand, he stared at the screen for a long moment before looking up. When their eyes met, some of the ice casing around her heart melted.

"Give me your address and I can have a crew there around the clock until we can arrive," he said.

That was the reason he stared at his phone? So he could get a crew to help her. She'd been one hundred percent certain the person on the other side of those texts was a woman a few seconds ago. A burn of embarrassment flamed her cheeks, turning them a couple of shades past red. She'd always disliked people who jumped to conclusions, which was exactly what she'd done. Emerson acknowledged the hit. She wouldn't make the same mistake twice.

After rattling off her address, she took the couple of steps toward him and reached for his forearm while the sheriff's deputy was on the phone giving information.

"I'm not sure how I'll repay all your kindness," she said to Rory. Her fingertips tingled from the contact.

"Not required," he said in his all-business tone. Had she hurt his feelings? Well, now she really did feel bad. She'd cold-shouldered him this morning, but to be honest, that was more for her own protection than anything else. Rory was intelligent, kind and had more honor in his pinkie finger than far too many other men had in their whole bodies. He was the kind of person she could see herself wanting to get to know better. Therein lay the problem. He was keeping secrets, or a secret.

She needed to get home before anyone got past Rory's crew. And she needed to find a way to thank Rory when this was all said and done.

"What else do you know about this break-in?" she asked. "Was anything else stolen?"

"Someone ran through the waiting area and overturned the coffee table," the deputy revealed. "After taking pictures, Jimmy set it upright and tossed the magazines back on top."

"Trying to make it look like a robbery," Rory said.

The deputy, Theo, nodded.

"Here's the thing," Jimmy interjected. "I have a cash box behind my counter, and no one bothered it." He threw his hands up. "It's the darnedest thing because I thought surely the break-in was for money. My petty cash was untouched. All four hundred dollars is still there."

Theo walked toward the door to the waiting area. He stopped in between rooms.

"Here's what I think," he began. "This doesn't fit the mold of the occasional vandalism, which makes me believe it was staged. Teens usually break in back windows and then run."

"They entered through the front," Rory repeated.

Theo squatted down. "If you look at the broken glass, it trails into the adjacent room."

"That's how you know they came in here," Rory reiterated. This whole line of conversation could literally make her sick. The fact someone had broken into Jimmy's with the sole purpose of finding out who she was and where she lived caused her stomach to churn.

Emerson followed the trail with her gaze. It made sense. The person or persons walked right over to the passenger side of her vehicle and must have used something to break into her vehicle. "The broken window explains how the person or persons got into the shop, but what about my Bronco? How did they get inside there when there are no broken windows?"

"That would be my fault." Jimmy stepped forward with a look of apology. "The person could have used a slim-jim on the lock, or if you look on the table right there next to the door, you'll find the key fob."

Emerson gasped.

"I couldn't be sorrier, ma'am." Jimmy hung his head. "In all the years I've owned this place and my father before me, there's never been a break-in. I got lazy by not locking up the keys. I just didn't think it could happen in a town like ours."

"You got comfortable," Emerson quickly corrected. She didn't want him feeling so awful for something he didn't do or see coming. "As it should be." Being from a city, she locked everything. Doors. Windows. Vehicle. She always knew where her purse was and kept a close eye on her cell phone when it wasn't in her hand or her bag. "There is something very nice about living in a place that doesn't always look over its shoulder or fear the worst all the time. It's actually kind of nice that you've never really had to worry when you really think about it."

"It's not much of a help right now," Jimmy said but at least his chin came up a bit. "Your home could be invaded because of my mistake."

"Rory and the deputy are working to make sure that doesn't happen," Emerson said. "And, besides, when you really think about it, I'm the one who brought this to your door. It's not your fault. If I hadn't come looking for the woman in the photo, none of this would have taken place. Please, don't beat yourself up over it."

Jimmy fisted his hands and placed them on his hips while he seemed to contemplate those words.

"The person you're looking for is your mother?" he asked. "Is that what I heard yesterday?"

"I believe so," Emerson said, folding her arms across her chest and rubbing them to stave off a sudden chill.

"It doesn't make sense, does it?" he asked her, scratching his head. "Why would that possibly cause so much trouble?"

"That seems to be the question of the day, Jimmy," she said. One she hoped to find answers to before anything else happened.

Jimmy walked the scene again, shaking his head as he retraced the steps. Theo's theory made sense. Someone made it look like a smash-and-grab job or teens getting into mischief. The place was in disarray. An arm swipe across the tops of surfaces was what the damage amounted to. Like a tall kindergartner ran through the room clearing tabletops without stopping before bolting out the door again. Whoever was behind it staged this to look random, so the person could get her address. Why?

"THE BASTARD BEHIND this must not have resources or contacts to run a license plate, which rules out dirty law enforcement because it would leave a trail." Rory was on the receiving end of quite a sour look after his comment. He put his hands up in the surrender position. "I'm not accusing deputies of illegal activity or insinuating they would do something like this. However, I don't know who is working for the law these days other than you so I'm not calling out anyone specifically. Ruling folks out by elimination gives us a few less names to put on the list. I'm just trying to cancel out groups if possible."

"I'd be shocked if anyone in town is responsible for this," Jimmy stated.

"And yesterday?" Rory asked. "What about that? The first incident circles back around to Bynum Ross. Then there was a truck parked outside the B&B last night, down the street."

A look passed between Jimmy and Theo that Rory didn't like.

"It's peculiar," Theo agreed. "I thought you were home to visit your family."

"This is a detour," Rory answered with finality in his tone. This wasn't something he wanted to keep talking about. Theo nodded in acquiescence.

"Let's review the facts," Rory said, growing more and more concerned about how quiet Emerson had been in the past few minutes. She stood to the side of the room with her arms folded across her chest like a barricade. She was studying the scene, assessing every detail so she could put an end to this once and for all. He was afraid it wasn't going to be so easy.

A vehicle pulled up in front of the building. Since Rory was near the front window, he was able to take a look without so much as taking a step. *Mother?*

Considering he hadn't been the one to make the call, he could only assume Doris had. What did she have to gain by distracting him? His cell picked that moment to chime, indicating a message was coming through.

"Excuse me," he said as his mother made a beeline for the front door. Talk about worlds colliding. His daughter was trying to call him while his mother—who didn't know she had a granddaughter—was about to walk through the door. As soon as he got out of earshot of Emerson, he answered Liv. "Is everything okay?"

"Yeah, hey, Dad." Liv's voice cut through the stress and had a way of calming him down. If she was happy, then all was all right in the world. He had no idea how long it would last, but this was her happy voice. He'd take it.

"Hey, kiddo," he said, taking in a slow breath.

"I was about to ask you the same question," she said. "You know. Like, is everything okay?"

"With me?" he asked. "Yes. I'm good."

"I know you're on a business trip right now, but you've been acting strange and I was just thinking..."

Liv could overthink a situation.

"Have I?" he asked. "Because I haven't meant to. I'm good. You know how business can be." It wasn't a complete lie. He had business to attend to. Business that was about to walk through the door. Again, he asked himself how life had gotten so complicated. One minute, he was a single father launching a successful business; the next, he was a juggler trying to keep everything from crashing down around him. "Why? Is everything okay on your end?"

"Sure," she said quickly. A little too quickly? "I mean, like, Maria's mother just got diagnosed with something like cancer of…" She sighed dramatically and his heart nearly ripped in two. "Anyway, she might not live and that got me thinking. What if something happened to you? Where would that leave me? I mean, it's just like the two of us and nothing can happen—"

"Hold on there, kitten. Nothing, and I mean *nothing*, is going to happen to me. I'm strong as an ox," he reassured her. Now he felt even more guilty for keeping Liv from the rest of his family. Duncan Hayes might have shamed a young Rory into leaving town, but he was a man now and needed to make this right. Besides, he'd thought the same thing more times than he wanted to count. What would happen to Liv if anything happened to him?

He couldn't go there because he would not leave his daughter alone in this world. Period.

"You don't know that," Liv said, her voice small and vulnerable.

Rather than lie to her, he came straight out with the truth.

"You know what?" he began. "You're right. I can't predict the future. But the one thing I know is that you would be fine. I've made sure of it and I'll be able to explain it all very soon. Okay?"

She hesitated but agreed.

"Just promise me that you're not going anywhere anytime soon," she said, and he could hear the fear in her voice. A popular African proverb said it took a village to raise a child. He had one with Cecile Welch, his neighbors and the school. Was that enough?

Rory was beginning to realize that it wasn't, but he hated Liv worrying about it. She needed to be focused on being a kid, and nothing else.

Was that reality?

"I'll do my best," he said. "Promise."

"Daaad," she said.

"Here's the thing, kiddo. I will always be honest with you. I don't have any idea what the future holds. All I can tell you is that, right now, I'm healthy as I've ever been. I get screened and tested six ways past Tuesday to make sure of it," he said. "But, if something should happen, I promise you with all my heart that you will not be alone in this world. Okay?"

"Okay," she said in the tone that reminded him underneath all that sass and eye rolling was a little girl. *His* little girl.

"Are we good?" he asked.

"Better," Liv stated.

"We've been happy, right?" he asked, wondering if there was a better life out there for her with a bigger family. "You've been okay?"

"Yeah, of course. Why? What happened?" she asked with an unsteady quality to her voice.

"Nothing," he said. "I just wanted to know if it's been good between us. You've had a good childhood, right?"

As much as he probably shouldn't be asking an

almost teenager those questions, he couldn't help himself.

"Yeeees," she said, really drawing out the word. He could tell that he was making her nervous about where this was going.

"That's all I need to know," he said, wondering if she would still feel the same way when he turned her world upside down with the news that was coming.

Chapter Eleven

Out of the corner of Emerson's eye, she watched the scene unfold outside as Rory met a woman old enough to be his mother in front of her SUV. The woman threw her arms around his midsection, and Emerson was almost certain the older woman wiped tears from her eyes.

"Is that Rory's mother?" she asked Jimmy.

"Yes, ma'am," he responded.

Wanting to give the mother and son their privacy, Emerson forced her gaze away.

"How long do you think it will take to fix my Bronco?" she asked, thinking she also needed to get what she needed from this place and move on. It might be safer for her to stay in a motel half an hour away from Cider Creek and then drive in during the day. She could check the map and figure out a way to take a different road out of town when she left, make sure no one followed her and double down on her investigation. At this point, she'd be willing to show her mother's picture to everyone in town and knock on the doors of everyone in the area to see if anyone was willing to talk.

"It'll be two to three days at a minimum," Jimmy said. "I'll do my best to get you fixed up and on the road as soon as humanly possible."

Emerson frowned. She couldn't imagine going two or three more days without a vehicle of her own. After the glimpse of mother and son, she couldn't allow Rory to stay with her when he needed to be visiting home like his original plan.

She pulled her cell phone out of her purse, determined to rent a car so as not to inconvenience him any longer. The B&B wasn't a good place for her to stay no matter how much she instantly liked Doris. Speaking of whom, Emerson needed to circle back around and ask the hostess about the photo too. Doris knew something and she was keeping it to herself. If Emerson had a chance at wearing the hostess down, she would make every effort. She would fall on Doris's mercy at this point.

"Have you investigated Bynum Ross?" she asked Theo as he joined her and Jimmy.

"I spoke to him last night but it's not my place to discuss the details of an ongoing investigation," Theo stated. Without Rory standing by her side, Theo wasn't looking nearly as warm and friendly. Jimmy seemed guarded too.

Had they been putting on an act? The thought left her unsettled. Did they know more than either of them was letting on?

For a long moment, she stood and stared into Theo's eyes. Eyes usually told her a whole lot about a person and their motive. His gave the impression that he was hiding something or holding back. If he'd interviewed Bynum last night, Theo learned something that he wasn't either at liberty or willing to say.

"Is he involved in this?" She waved her hand. "Is he responsible? Because there is no way you can convince me it had been an accident when that truck tried to run me off the road last night."

Theo leaned back on his heels and tucked his hands in his front pockets. "I'm not trying to." His stern expression softened a little bit. "I'm sorry that happened to you." He let out a frustrated sigh. She knew that his loyalties would be to folks in Cider Creek, not some random outsider. Did she think he was capable of looking the other way when laws were being broken? She didn't know. Would he have more sympathy toward the side of a story being told by a local? She'd bet money on it.

The sound of the SUV pulling away caused her to look over in the direction of the parking lot. Rory stood there, alone. There was no phone in his hand as he waved. This seemed like a good time to have a conversation with him, so she walked out of the room and approached.

"Hey," he said after turning around. With his beautiful and kind eyes directly focused on her, she wasn't so certain she could say what was on her mind.

She dropped her gaze, cleared her throat and refocused. This situation wasn't fair to him or his family. "We need to talk." At least she'd gotten that much out.

"Yes, we do," he said in a surprise move. She looked up to find him studying her.

"You first," she offered.

"The woman who just showed up here was my mother," he said. "As I've mentioned before, we haven't seen each other in a very long time. Someone called her, she wouldn't say who, and let the cat out of the bag that I was in town. My mom called the inn, and Doris let her know where I'd headed off to. She also mentioned you to my mom."

"Oh. I wonder why she did that." Emerson really was confused.

"Here's the thing about the good folks in this town—they want to help," he stated. "So, my mom drove over here the minute after she initiated the call to Doris to invite you to stay at the ranch."

Emerson blinked a couple of times. This couldn't be real. Could it?

"I don't know if that's a good idea," she argued without a whole lot of enthusiasm. "In fact, I was just checking my phone to find a rental car. You came home for a reason that didn't involve me and you've gone above and beyond the call of duty to help, but I don't feel right asking for more."

He stood there for a long moment.

"Okay, understood," he said in another surprise move. She half expected him to try to talk her out of that line of thinking and was more than a little disappointed he didn't. Her reaction caught her off guard.

"I am so appreciative of everything you've done so far," she continued. "There's no way that I would have made it through the night without your help. And now you're sending a crew to make sure my house isn't broken into."

He nodded.

"Anytime," he responded. "They worked out a rotation, so someone is always there. We can keep that going as long as needed."

"That's great actually," she said. He was saying everything she thought she wanted him to say, so why didn't it feel great? The reason dawned on her almost immediately. Because this meant they were saying goodbye. She glanced toward the building to make sure Jimmy and Theo weren't within earshot. "I'm concerned Theo isn't as objective as he might think he is. I've decided not to stay in Cider Creek."

"Okay," he said, his gaze intensifying on her.

"I think it might be for the best," she said. "I'm figuring that I can take a different way back to my hotel in the hopes no trucks follow me." She shivered at the thought of what had happened yesterday on the road and with the truck that was parked outside the B&B. Actually, they had no proof the second truck was there to watch her, but the timing had been quite a coincidence.

"Sounds like you've thought all of this through," he said, crossing his arms over a broad chest.

Hearing it as she said it out loud, she realized how lonely it sounded. The deck also seemed to be stacked against her in Cider Creek. Asking around could prove dangerous.

"I probably need to make an appointment to speak to the sheriff just to let him know what has been happening and that I have a few safety concerns," she said. "I'm probably going to need to bring him into the investigation at this point."

"That's reasonable," he said. "My family knows him. We could make a call. My family name should open a few more doors for you in and around town."

"I'd like that a lot actually," she said. "Showing the picture to one person sure did kick up a dust storm." She made eyes at him, realizing this might be bigger than she wanted to accept or acknowledge. Turning a blind eye could be dangerous, though, and she was starting to wonder if she was making the right calls.

"We can do this any way you want," he said with a calm tone that sent his deep timbre right through her. A voice should be heard and not felt. "No one is trying to force anything on you, and I don't want to pressure you into something you wouldn't be comfortable with." And then he looked at her with uncertainty and maybe a little bit of concern in his eyes. "Is that what you really want? Or is that the way you think it should go because you're too kind to put anyone else out."

When he put it in those words, she had to think about it for a second.

"Because you honestly don't have to do any of this alone, Emerson." The way her name rolled off his tongue sent more of those vibrations through her, warming her. "Either way, it's your call."

It didn't feel like a conscious choice.

"I don't want to interfere with whatever you have going on with your family," she said, but that wasn't the only thing bugging her about spending more time with him. She was scared to lean on him. "And you have a secret."

She hadn't meant to blurt out the last part, but it was too late to take it back now.

RORY DIDN'T HAVE a clue what she was talking about. There was no secret that impacted her. Until his cell buzzed and Emerson made a subtle face. She recovered so fast that for a split second, he believed he'd imagined it. And in another, he almost told her about Liv. If the information would help Emerson make a decision to allow him and his family to help, it would be worth it. His mother would understand and, knowing her, would probably do the same thing under the circumstances.

"Does my phone have anything to do with the secret that you're concerned about?" he asked, realizing she must believe he had a serious girlfriend or wife tucked away somewhere.

She hesitated and, for a moment, he wasn't certain

she would answer. Then came, "Yes. But I also want to say that it wouldn't be any of my business except there were a couple of kisses that maybe shouldn't have happened even though they were incredible." Her cheeks flamed at the admission, and it only made her more beautiful than before. It also occurred to him that she deserved an explanation. He hadn't considered how all those phone calls and texts might look to someone else, and it was obvious to him that he hadn't been in a relationship in so long that he'd forgotten a few courtesies. Not that the two of them were in a relationship per se. To be fair, they had kissed and the kisses had been flaming hot.

Since a picture was worth a thousand words, he fished out his cell phone and held out the screen so Emerson could see it.

"My daughter," he said. "Before I give you the details, these guys have no idea about her, and I'd like to keep it that way until I have a conversation with my mother."

Her eyebrows drew together in confusion. And then a whole conversation played out across her features.

He put his hand up, palm out.

"I'm not trying to sway your decision. However, if you'd like to come home to the ranch with me, you could line up all your resources from there. There'd be a laptop for you to use, which might make researching a little easier on the eyes," he informed. There. He'd laid his cards on the table and now it was her turn to make the call. He'd done what he could to explain.

"Okay, that sounds good," she said. "It'll give me a chance to regroup and figure out my next steps while the Bronco is fixed." Her eyes sparkled when she said, "Your daughter is beautiful, by the way."

He exhaled the breath he'd been holding as Theo and Jimmy joined them.

"Thank you," he said quietly, so only she could hear as the others approached.

"I'll file my report and be in touch if we need anything else," Theo said.

"Sounds good," Rory said, reclaiming his casual demeanor. "Just so you know, we're planning to meet with the sheriff later to discuss the details of what has been happening." Theo needed to know exactly what Rory was planning because he suspected Emerson was correct. Someone like Bynum Ross might be able to intimidate Theo.

"If that's what you need to do," Theo said, sounding resigned.

"These events are connected," Rory stated, leaving it at that. He'd planted a seed.

Theo studied the ground, causing alarm bells to sound in Rory's mind.

"We'll be taking off unless you need us for anything else," Rory continued. "Don't hesitate to call me or the ranch if you need more information or have any questions."

Theo nodded and Rory noticed the chill in the air now.

"No, sir," Theo said.

Jimmy offered an apologetic look. He shrugged.

"Do you need help with cleanup?" Rory asked.

"Nah," Jimmy said with a wave. "I got this."

"Holler if you need anything," Rory said to Jimmy.

"You know I will," he said. "I've got to get inside and clean up so I can get to working on Ms. Emerson's Bronco."

After saying their goodbyes, Rory and Emerson reclaimed their seats inside his truck. Once they were settled and on the road, he said, "Thank you for trusting me."

"It's a two-way street," she said.

"I promised that I'd tell you about my daughter," he said, picking up the conversation where it left off before they'd been interrupted.

"You don't have to," Emerson said. "I didn't have any business calling you out earlier."

"It's fine," he defended. "You made good points. We'd kissed and, besides, I wanted to come clean about the cell phone situation. It took you mentioning something for me to realize how that might look."

"I understand now," she said.

"Then, you won't mind me explaining my past," he said. "And why I didn't immediately want to talk about my situation."

Chapter Twelve

In a million years, Emerson never would have guessed all those phone calls and text had come from a daughter. "It's complicated" was about to be explained.

"We were about to graduate high school when my daughter was conceived," he said. "We'd been high school sweethearts and I firmly believed we would spend the rest of our lives together."

It was so much easier to fall hard for someone before anyone knew how bad the pain would be if it didn't work out. First loves rarely made it the distance, but they were very sweet. Hers had been a boy by the name of Austin Charles. Looking back, they'd shared an adorable crush, but her father would never have allowed the two of them to spend any real time together. It had been a flirtation that had ended when Valerie, a cheerleader, had set her sights on Austin.

"Funny how *forever* is such an easy word to throw around at that age," she commiserated.

"Sure is," he agreed.

"You broke up, but you never came home?" she asked. "I would think you would need family more than ever with a little one."

"I did," he said. "My grandfather shamed us out of town. Being a headstrong eighteen-year-old, I decided that Leah—that was her name—and I could handle anything together."

"I can imagine having a well-known family would put a lot more pressure on you than a normal person," she said, especially after the way she saw folks here in Cider Creek treat him like the prodigal son.

"My grandfather convinced me my mother would be devastated by the pregnancy, and hurting her was the last thing I wanted to do." She could hear the pain in his voice.

"We can make rash decisions when we're that young," she said.

"Don't I know it. When taking care of a baby became too much for Leah, she bolted and hasn't looked back."

"Is that the reason she gave when she left?" she asked.

"In a nutshell," he stated. "Looking back, I would handle everything a whole lot differently with my family."

"That's just it, though, isn't it? Learning from mistakes helps us become the people we're meant to be." She heard in his tone how much he was still beating himself up. "At eighteen, we don't exactly make the best choices and there's a reason for that.

We start to think we're grown and have no idea what the real world is like or how our decisions might impact us years later."

"That's true," he said after a thoughtful pause. "I can handle my own mistakes and how it hurt me. I'm starting to realize how hurt my mother will be once she finds out I've been withholding her grandchild all these years. My father died years ago, and she stayed on at her father-in-law's ranch even though Duncan Hayes was a jerk." He tightened his grip on the steering wheel. "I've deprived my daughter of the family she deserved to grow up with and that's not fair to her. To any of them."

"First of all, I'm sorry for your loss. I may not have known you your entire life. In fact, we've only really just met even though it seems odd to me because it feels like I've known you for so much longer." She shook off the thought, unsure if she was even making sense. "But you would never hurt someone else intentionally."

"Doesn't change the fact that I have."

"No," she said. "You're right. It doesn't and that's where an apology comes in."

"It won't erase the damage," he said.

"Right again," she said. "Beating yourself up over the past doesn't, either."

His gaze intensified on the stretch of road in front of them. Her comment seemed to score a direct hit.

Emerson's heart went out to his daughter, though. Not because of anything Rory had done wrong. In her book, he'd been a saint. Emerson was all too familiar with growing up without a female influence in her life.

"The job is too important to get wrong," he finally said.

"Sounds like you're taking it seriously," she said. "How old is Liv?"

"Almost thirteen," he said.

"Oh, tough age." She noticed how his face lit up now when he talked about his daughter.

"She's a good kid and, believe me, I know how lucky I am that she likes school and does well." More of that pride came out in his voice. He cracked a smile too. "She's quick and that makes her a handful sometimes."

"Sounds like a dream," she said. She'd dated an older man once who was a single dad. His kids were young, ages four and six. The mother was in the picture, so Emerson's heart didn't hurt for the kids in the way it did for Liv. "You're doing an amazing job."

"I got lucky with her," he quickly countered.

"Maybe." She figured this wasn't the time to argue with the man about his parenting skills even though he seemed to be selling himself short. The love he had for his daughter was evident in everything he said. Liv was a lucky young lady to have someone care so much about her.

"We're almost home," he said, changing the subject.

"To the right?" she asked. All she could see was

fence and field. A house wasn't visible by the road, blocked by trees. To the left was a small subdivision with decent-sized yards.

"Yes," he said. "You'll see the main house once we get onto the property. My grandfather liked his privacy."

A gate protected the drive, which was another sign she was probably in over her head with this family. Halfway down the drive, the main house came into view just like he'd promised.

"Whoa," was all she could think to say. She'd never been inside an actual mansion before, but this place had all the grandeur of one. A small gravel lot sat beside the home, if it could be called that. "I'm way out of my league here."

"It can be overwhelming at first, but you get used to it after a while," Rory said.

"There's no way," she said quietly. She couldn't imagine ever feeling comfortable inside those walls.

The SUV from earlier was parked in the spot closest to the palatial home. The place itself was intimidating. She could only imagine what his grandfather had been like.

"What about your siblings? Do they still live here?" She wanted to know what she might be walking into.

"Oh, no," he said with a head shake as he parked beside the SUV. "Our grandfather caused everyone to want to leave. My oldest brother, Callum, bolted out even before I did. There are six of us in total. Four boys and two girls. Last time I talked to my brother, everyone left the second they could. They all split off in different directions. I should probably warn you that my mother has asked everyone to come home and take our rightful places working the ranch."

"Is that what any of you want?" she asked.

"Callum owns a logistics business. He moves different products around the country from warehouse or dock to stores. He's based in Houston but met Payton on his recent trip home, so now he splits his time between the two cities. All of sudden, he's engaged. I don't have all the details yet, but he's the only one in the family who knows about Liv. Once Leah left, I was too ashamed to come home. Back then, all I wanted to do was become a success so when I returned to Cider Creek it wouldn't be as a failure. I would be able to hold my head up high and not bring shame to my mother. Once Leah left, I didn't think that would be possible ever again. Then, too much time passed, and I didn't know how to go back. Does that make any sense?"

She realized he'd dovetailed the conversation back to why he hadn't come home in all these years. Facing his mother with the news he had coming—a mother he seemed to love and respect—must be one of the most difficult things he'd ever done.

"She'll forgive you," Emerson said, looking him in the eyes—eyes that were filled with uncertainty and hurt despite a tough exterior. Her heart went out to him. Rory Hayes stirred emotions she wasn't quite ready to face but didn't want to walk away from either. "I promise she will."

Before she acted on instinct and leaned over to kiss him, she exited the passenger side.

RORY CIRCLED AROUND the front of the truck, and then reached for Emerson's hand. She tensed at the contact but almost immediately relaxed. Did she feel the same jolt of electricity he did when they touched? Her reaction right now made him think so. His ego wouldn't allow him to say she hadn't enjoyed their few kisses as much as he had. Then again, that was a tall order because they'd ranked up there with the best in his life to date. If he was being totally honest, they were the best. Right now, he didn't want to go there with what it might mean.

He didn't let go of her hand until he had to reach for the back door.

The kitchen was as grand as he remembered it to be. A massive granite island anchored the room. The place looked like a professional chef's work area. The farmhouse sink sat below a window that overlooked the backyard and barns. There were two side-by-side stainless steel fridges. An oven with more doors than he knew what to do with when he lived here let alone now. It looked like a baker's paradise, though. A long wooden table that seated a dozen comfortably was against the back wall.

"How about another cup of coffee while I track down my mother?" he suggested.

Before Emerson could answer, his mother came rushing into the room in all of her five-foot, two-inch glory.

"Rory," she said, then her gaze shifted to Emerson.

"This is the friend I was telling you about at Jimmy's," he said as his mother beamed up at him. She was one of those fiery redheads folks claimed were full of spit and vinegar, but she was actually calm and had the kind of warmth people were drawn to, like a campfire on a chilly night. He figured that was where the reputation came from.

"You must be Emerson," his mother said. She brought Emerson into a hug.

"Mrs. Hayes," Emerson said with an emotion present he couldn't quite put his finger on. It dawned on him that she might never have truly been hugged by a mother, any mother, in her entire life. A coil tightened in his chest at the thought, not just for Emerson but for his daughter as well. Would Liv have the same reaction to a motherly embrace? Would she have to fight back tears in the same way Emerson was doing?

Before he could get too far down that road, Granny came bopping into the kitchen. Not much had changed about her, and he was all the more grateful for it. She even looked about the same age as she had all those years ago when he'd left town for good. Gray hair piled on top of her head in a knot, smile as bright and wide as the Texas sky, Granny was a force. She rubbed her eyes in dramatic fashion.

"Rory Hayes!"

"Yes, ma'am," he said, returning the smile. Being in this house without Duncan Hayes was strange. The air was lighter somehow. His grandfather walked around in a dark cloud of criticism and crankiness. There was a heaviness when he was in the room.

Rory met Granny halfway across the room and gave her a hug. She had on one of her flannel gowns that she was famous for. Socks and slippers rounded out the outfit.

"Good to have you home," Granny said and when she pulled back from the hug, she had watery eyes.

"I missed you more than you could know," he said to her.

"The cards and flowers have been nice. No return address made it impossible to thank you, though," she scolded.

"No thanks was ever necessary," he said as flippantly as he could manage under the circumstances. The rubber was about to meet the road on his deception. The weight of holding on to the secret had nearly dragged him to the ocean floor. "Besides, you could have done an internet search if you'd wanted to."

"Figured you'd come home when you were ready. Hell would freeze over before I'd push myself where I wasn't wanted," Granny quipped.

"Would you like something to drink?" his mother, Marla, asked Emerson, interrupting the moment.

Granny had a smile on her face, so she didn't mean any harm with the comment.

"Is coffee too much trouble?" she asked.

"Not at all," his mother said, waving her off like it was nothing. "Did you eat?"

"Doris made breakfast," Rory said. "Why don't the three of you sit down at the table while I pour?"

His mother stopped and then turned around, making a beeline for the table instead. She was on edge and he wondered how much she was picking up on his emotions. Or had it been so long since he'd been home that she didn't know how to act around him any longer?

"I owe you an apology," his mother began after taking a seat next to Emerson. Granny took the head of the table. He figured it was easier for her to get in and out of the chair.

"For what?" he asked, wondering what on earth she thought she'd done. From his vantage point, she'd been an angel, which made him even more frustrated with his grandfather.

"Not making this a safe place to come home to," she immediately said, wringing her hands together.

"What? You?" The thought she could have been blaming herself all these years gutted him. Before she could answer, he said, "Believe me when I say that you did nothing wrong."

"I've spoken to Callum," she said solemnly before turning to Emerson. "I'm sorry you have to hear this when we should be celebrating Rory coming home.

I just can't let another minute go by without apologizing for not making this an easier place to come home to."

"You weren't the problem," Rory said with a whole lot of emphasis on the first word in the sentence.

"Even so," she said. "I should have realized and I didn't."

"You were a saint for putting up with six kids, and a father-in-law who was a…" He stopped himself from finishing.

His mother let her breath out in a long sigh. "Some of the things Duncan said to Callum… I had no idea he was being such a jerk. I thought it was good for you guys to have a male role model around after losing your father even though I realized Duncan was far from perfect."

His father had died out of the blue in a car crash shortly after Rory started high school.

"I stayed on because I missed him so much and this place reminded me of him," she admitted. "But if I'd known Duncan was being a complete jerk to you guys…"

Granny placed her hand on top of his mother's.

"I've told you already that wasn't your fault," Granny said.

"I didn't protect my children and now none want to come home," his mother said. "How is that not my fault?"

Rory finished filling four mugs before bringing them all over to the table. He sat one down in front of each person before taking a seat across the table with the last one. "Parents make mistakes all the time."

His mother glanced at him with a look that said she appreciated the thought but he couldn't possibly know what she was talking about. He was about to have news for her.

Chapter Thirteen

"I have a daughter."

Emerson did her best not to stare at anyone after Rory dropped his bomb. The rim of her coffee mug became real interesting to her about then.

"Oh?" Marla said. The mix of confusion and curiosity in her voice made Emerson wonder what her mother was going to say when she showed up at the door unannounced after all these years. Presumably, her mother didn't know if Emerson was alive or dead. Did she care? Or had she been kept in the dark?

"Her name is Liv," he continued as his grandmother picked her jaw up from the table.

"When did this happen?" Marla asked as confusion knitted her eyebrows together. "What I mean to ask is, how old is she?"

"Twelve," he said.

"Months?" Marla asked.

He shook his head and his shame was written all over his face as he searched his mother's face. "Years."

Marla's gaze dipped down to his hand, third finger on the left. "Are you…?"

"No." He shook his head as though for emphasis. "Not married. Not any longer anyway."

"Okay, I'm sorry to hear that, Rory," Marla was still walking lightly around the subject. To her credit, she didn't freak out or start bombing him with questions. She did, however, look at Emerson. "Are you two…?"

Emerson shook her head a little too emphatically because his grandmother's eyebrow shot up.

"This is just a friend," Rory explained. It was true and yet those words stung.

"I'm in a bind and your son is helping me out," Emerson explained.

"You've been awfully quiet, Granny," Rory said.

"Uh-huh," she confirmed.

"Are you still speaking to me?" he asked.

"Uh-huh," she reassured. Now, she started lightly tapping her index finger on the table and Emerson wasn't certain if it was a good or bad sign.

"Tell me about her," Marla said with a warmth in her eyes that warmed Emerson's heart.

"She's spunky, like Granny here, and smart like you," Rory said with the kind of parental pride that almost made Emerson tear up. "Of course, I'm biased but she's a beautiful kid."

"Do you have a picture?" Marla asked, but he was already fishing through his cell phone.

"Here she is," he said, chest out, smile wide. He

held out the cell first for his mother to see and then to his grandmother.

Emerson caught a glimpse of his daughter and thought the young girl was beautiful.

"You'll have to beat the boys off with a stick," his grandmother said. "She's a beauty."

"Don't tell me that," he warned, but it was all pride coming through in his voice. "She's smart. Gets solid grades and doesn't get into trouble."

Marla sat quietly studying the picture. She seemed to be doing the math in her head. Then came, "Leah?"

He nodded and his mother seemed to catch on. She reached over and touched his other hand reassuringly.

"I'm sorry it didn't work out," she said.

"Turns out, she didn't think she was cut out to be a mother after all," he said. "Of course, it was a little too late by the time she realized it."

"Is she involved in Liv's life at all?" Marla asked.

He gave a slight head shake.

"When you were talking about making mistakes as a parent a few minutes ago, I just need you to know that I think you're an incredible mother," he said. Tears streamed down all three of their faces.

His grandmother coughed and then excused herself to the bathroom. Obviously, she wasn't one to show her emotions. Since this seemed like a mother-son moment, Emerson excused herself to go outside. There was no way she could keep from bawling if she'd stayed inside a minute longer. Cool air hit her the second she stepped into the breeze. Air was good. She needed air. Witnessing the intimate family moment had threatened to shatter more of the casing around her heart. She'd never seen so much tenderness, remorse and subsequent understanding in a family before. Her father might have loved her, but he'd taken overprotective to a whole new level.

Looking back, she couldn't imagine surprising him with news of anything of this magnitude without him blowing a gasket. There would have been screaming and cursing, blaming. She'd spent a good portion of her childhood walking on eggshells, and yet it had all been so normal to her back then. She'd made a game out of being alone. There'd been plenty of books around. Her father would have flipped out if she'd gotten on social media but he wasn't opposed to books. It wasn't until she thought back to those days after experiencing freedom did she realize how suffocating much of her early childhood had been. And lonesome. Kids were adaptable, though. She'd molded her life to fit the circumstances.

Growing up here at the ranch with all this open space would have been incredible. Emerson was in awe of the beauty of the land here. It was a sanctuary. Funny how one person had made it impossible for Rory and his siblings to stay despite his love of the property and, clearly, his mother and grandmother. Her heart went out to him. No one wanted to disappoint the people they loved most. Call it cowboy code, but Rory Hayes was the most honorable person she'd met. She could only imagine the pain he must have felt at the thought of bringing shame to his family.

Taking a seat on an Adirondack chair that faced the large yard, Emerson finally relaxed. Out here, she didn't want to think about the damage to her Bronco or the fact she was probably an orphan now. She set aside everything else for a moment so she could just breathe. The crisp air out here was so clean. The breeze carried a hint of wildflowers in its earthy scent.

The sun warmed her face as she closed her eyes and tried her best to clear her mind. Focusing on a problem always seemed to push the solution further away. Who needed a spa when they had all this? Emerson could sit here for days and a growing piece of her wished she could leave her old life behind, repress the need to find her mother and just breathe.

Except she realized it wouldn't work. The opposite was happening. The more folks put up roadblocks in her search, the more determined she became to bust them down.

The door opened and Rory emerged. She craned her neck around and was met with a concerned look.

"Is everything all right?" she asked as dread filled her at the thought of more bad news.

"I have to go," he said.

"Is Liv all right?" Her mind immediately snapped to something bad happening to his daughter.

"Yes, she's fine. A second one of my construction sites caught fire and I need to see the damage for myself."

Emerson was already pushing to standing. "Where?"

"In Dallas."

"Mind if I ride shotgun?" she asked, thinking she could rent a vehicle while she was there. From the sounds of it, he was going to need to handle business for a while. He might even need to pull his crew from babysitting her home. They could discuss it on the drive.

"Are you sure you don't want to hang around here?" he asked. "You'll have access to one of the work trucks, and my mom already offered to let you stay in the main house. There's security here at the ranch."

"One hundred percent certain," she stated, shaking her head before he could finish his sentence. "We can talk on the road." She glanced around and realized she'd left her purse hanging on the back of her chair at the kitchen table. "I'll just be a second."

Emerson bolted into the kitchen, figuring there was no time to waste. They needed to get on the road. Dallas was probably at least a five-hour drive from here, and that's if traffic conditions were favorable.

Granny was back at the table while Marla was busy setting up to cook something.

"It was lovely meeting both of you," Emerson said as she made her way to her handbag.

"You're going to Dallas?" Granny asked. Her expression was far more concerned than when they'd met a little while ago. Rory had dropped a bomb on his grandmother and Marla, and they seemed to be processing the news without anger or judgment.

"Yes, ma'am," Emerson said.

"Good," his grandmother said, looking at least a little relieved now.

"I'm glad Rory will have such a good—" Marla managed a smile "—friend with him. Thank you."

"I may not have known your son for very long, but I can see how much your support means to him," she said to Marla. "It's not my place to say, but I know how much he's been agonizing and beating himself up over how everything transpired."

"We've already forgiven him. He was protecting me and his daughter the best way he knew how," Marla said. "Only a perfect mother can pass judgment on someone else, and I can assure you no one in this house falls into that category."

Emerson paused in the middle of the kitchen for a long moment.

"You know, I've always believed perfect was about the most boring thing a person could try to be," she said. "Messy, honest, good. Those are far better qualities in a person. Don't you think?"

Marla crossed the kitchen, and then brought her into a warm hug.

"Thank you," was all she said and she finally exhaled. "My son is lucky to have you in his life."

"I'm pretty certain the opposite is true, but I appreciate the compliment," Emerson said.

"Have a safe trip," Marla stated with the kind of warmth that made Emerson want to lean into.

After goodbyes, she headed toward the truck and Rory as he fired the engine up. Was she going to meet his daughter today? The thought caused all of her nerves to tense up. A twelve-year-old's impression of Emerson had never felt so important.

Rory white-knuckled the steering wheel as Emerson took the passenger seat.

"Don't worry about dropping me off anywhere once we get to Dallas," she said to him as he navigated out of the gravel lot and onto the long driveway. "I know you'll be busy on the site and I'm fine with figuring things out on my own."

If she thought she was lightening his load, the offer only served to frustrate him more. Yes, he was in a bad mood, but the comment rubbed him the wrong way. Since he'd been all about opening up and communicating a little while ago, he must still be in the zone because he couldn't let it go.

"Why are you always doing that?" he asked, forcing a calm that he didn't feel.

"What?" She sounded genuinely confused, which made him think she wasn't feeling the growing bond between them.

"Figuring out an exit plan," he stated. "If you don't want my help, that's…whatever. I told you that I'd like to see this through because I think you're in danger and in need of a friend. To tell you the truth, I could use one too. Especially of the female variety because I can't help but draw parallels to my daughter and what you've gone through. Are *still* going through. But here's the deal—I respect however you want to handle your own business. I just thought we did a decent job navigating through it together."

There. He'd said his piece.

"I wasn't really looking at it that way, to be honest," she said after a thoughtful pause. "The way I saw the situation is that you had other things to do and handle but couldn't because you were too busy being polite with me."

"Then what will it take for you to be convinced this is coming from me and not obligation?" he asked.

"That's it," she said, sounding a little more than surprised. "You just did it."

"Good," he concluded. "Because I do want to help you and not out of a sense of obligation but because I think you can use a friend as much as I can. I happen to think talking to you is easy and I don't know about you, but that's rare for me."

She seemed to let those words soak in.

"You brought up a good point," she started. "The part about me being ready to bolt and move on." She paused for a couple of beats. "I never really thought about it before. It's true, though. I'm just so used to being on my own that I'm not very good at being any other way. I guess you could say that I don't let people in, not coworkers, not people I interact with on an almost daily basis. I 'know' people without really being close to anyone."

More of that silence passed.

"The wild part is that I actually like you a lot. I enjoy talking to you and I'm not sure how I would have gotten through the past twenty-four hours without your help," she continued. "And I think maybe that spooks me a little bit."

"Because…?"

"What about when you're not here?" she asked. "What will I do then?"

"I'm here," he reassured. "I have no plans to go anywhere. Plus, I live in Mesquite and you live in Arlington. That's an almost straight shot across I-30. Without traffic, I'm there in less than an hour."

Out of the corner of his eye, he saw her nodding.

"Okay," she said. "No more talk about dropping me off. You want to help me see this through—I won't put up a fight anymore. Promise me one thing, though."

"Anything," he said. "Name it."

"Your business is our priority too," she said.

"That's a no brainer," he said. "We cover both at one time."

For reasons he didn't want to examine too closely, he wanted Emerson to meet Liv. And he hoped Liv liked her as much as he did.

Chapter Fourteen

The rest of the ride to the construction site seemed to fly by now that the air had been cleared. Emerson realized at the beginning of the trip she had never stopped to think about how she might be pushing others away before. Then again, she was certain she'd never met anyone like Rory. He was worth battling those fears that said everyone left eventually.

Change was the only constant. She needed to find a way to embrace it rather than try to direct something that was never in her control anyway.

They pulled up onto the small cordoned-off commercial site, where Rory parked the truck outside of the red-and-white tape. It was late and already getting dark. They hadn't stopped to eat, so they'd made good time. Emerson's stomach was beginning to feel the lack of food.

"If you trust me with your truck, I can go find food," she said to Rory. "That way, you can talk to the men and get a better sense of what happened here."

Rory nodded. "Sounds like a plan." He shook his head. "I have no idea how long we'll be here."

A slightly older woman wearing jeans, boots and a hard hat spotted him and immediately shifted position, heading right toward them.

"That's my right hand. She came to start the insurance claim," he said. "Her name is Cecile Welch and I'd be lost without her."

"Go handle whatever you need to and I'll bring back hot food," she said.

"Okay," Rory said before exiting the truck. She climbed over to the driver's seat without getting out of the vehicle. As she adjusted the seat, she heard a tap on the window. She turned to see the most intense set of eyes staring back at her. A lightning bolt struck the center of her chest. She pushed the button to lower the window since it looked like he had something important to say.

Then he cocked his head to one side.

"Never mind," he said.

"I'll be back in a few minutes," she promised.

He compressed his lips like he was holding back something he wanted to say before taking a step away and waving for her to go on. She backed out of the parking spot in time to see a young girl who looked to be about twelve to thirteen years old gunning toward him. She assumed this must be Liv.

Emerson's heart twisted at witnessing the father-daughter hug. Talk about warming her heart. Norman Rockwell couldn't paint a sweeter picture of today's

America than a rancher-turned-business-owner single father being tender with his soon-to-be-teenage girl.

A horn blasted behind her, and she realized the light had changed to green. She did her best to shake off the sweet image of father and daughter. Besides, Emerson was about to meet Liv and her insides were turned out at the possibility of the preteen taking an instant dislike to her. She had never been so nervous to meet anyone in her life.

As she got her bearings, she searched for fast food. She figured burgers would do the trick for now. There were plenty of burger-and-shake places in the area, so she picked the first one she came across and bought enough food to feed a small army. She got three flavors of milkshakes too.

It was completely dark outside by the time she made it back to the construction site. November usually meant chilly weather, and long nights. She cut the lights off and parked, figuring she might want to stay put. Rory had to have seen and heard her as she reentered the lot.

The building had burned down to studs. Rory's back was to her as he surveyed the damage. His daughter hugged his waist as he stood next to Cecile, his office manager.

All three turned around as she cut off the engine. There were a few nods before Rory broke off and Liv reached for Cecile's hand. The two headed off in a different direction than Rory, who came walking up. She scooted over into the passenger seat and he slid inside the truck. Her stomach growled as he claimed the driver's seat.

"I bought enough burgers for everyone," Emerson said. "I wasn't sure who'd eaten yet."

Rory turned to her and locked gazes. The moment their eyes connected, her heart dropped. There were no words to describe the look on his face.

"You brought food for my daughter?" he asked like he wasn't used to such kindness. It was a shame too because he thought of everyone else but himself.

"I wasn't sure if she likes burgers or milkshakes," she said with a shrug, trying to deflect some of the intensity of emotion in the moment. "I got every kind in case she was picky."

"Hold on a sec, okay?" he asked but he was already hopping out of the driver's side. He grabbed his cell phone and made a call. "Hey, Liv. I have someone here I'd like you to meet. Her name is Emerson and she picked up a burger and milkshake for you." He said a couple of uh-huhs into the phone before telling her to ask Cecile to swing around to the truck.

Emerson exited the truck on the passenger side and came around to where he stood. She crossed her arms over her chest to warm against the cool temperature. The next thing she knew, headlights were trained on the back of the truck and then a two-door sports car pulled up. Liv beamed from the passenger side. She eagerly hopped out of the vehicle, or should Emerson say climbed up and out of. How anyone rode in a sports car was beyond her. They might look cool, and they did, but she felt like she was sitting on top of the road when she rode inside them. Give her the Bronco any day of the week even though the red Camaro was a whole lot flashier of a ride.

"Liv, this is my friend Emerson," Rory said.

"Hey," Liv said before sticking her hand out.

"Hi," Emerson said with a handshake. "I wasn't sure what flavor milkshake you like, so I got all three."

Liv gasped and clapped her hands at the center of her chest. Tiny claps like she was trying to contain her excitement. Suddenly, she seemed like a little kid with the ear-to-ear grin on her face. Emerson was beginning to understand what Rory meant by Liv seeming older one minute and like a little kid the next with no warning in between. "Strawberry, please."

"Burger, cheeseburger or bacon cheeseburger?" Emerson continued, proud of the small progress she was making with the preteen.

"Bacon cheeseburger," she said as more of a question.

"Waffle or spiral fries?" Emerson asked the last question.

"Spiral. Always," she said.

"I happen to agree," Emerson said, grateful for the small thing they had in common. She turned and dug out the order before handing the items over to the girl. Liv's long straight hair fell past her shoulders. She had on a hoodie that would fit her father but somehow doubted it belonged to him. The words

Do What Makes You Happy, written in pink glitter, were a pretty good clue.

"Thank you," Liv practically chirped.

"Homework comes first before video games," Rory stated.

"Daaaad." Liv really dragged out the word. She fell short of an eye roll, though, but it came through in her tone of voice.

Emerson had to suppress the urge to laugh.

"Of course, I'll do my homework," she groaned. "When have I not done my homework?"

"Fine," he conceded. "Go eat before your food gets cold."

"The milkshake is supposed to be cold." Liv made a face and Emerson had to hold in her laugh. The kid was funny. Being around her made Emerson forget her own problems for a minute. "When are you coming home?"

"A couple of days," he said. "And I'll have a big surprise, so it'll be worth the wait."

This kid was about to meet a grandmother and great-grandmother who most people would trade an arm to call family. The thought stirred mixed emotions in Emerson. After spending twelve years believing her father was the only family she had, the kid was about to get a real treat.

"Bye, Dad," Liv said before turning her full attention to Emerson. "Nice to meet you." She held up the bag of food a little higher. "And thank you."

Emerson smiled and said, "You're welcome."

No one had ever captured Emerson's heart so quickly. But Liv was no ordinary kid.

She disappeared into the red sports car. Cecile seemed careful not to speed away.

"Liv's a good kid," she said to Rory. Before she could get too caught up in the emotions tugging at her heartstrings when she looked into his eyes, she added, "We should eat while it's still hot."

RORY WOLFED DOWN two burgers and a handful of fries before he realized how starved he'd been.

"I figured we could head over to your place and check to make sure all is good, maybe even grab a good night's sleep before we head back to Cider Creek tomorrow morning," he offered.

"Sounds good to me," she said. "All I can hope is that nothing exciting has gone on at my place. In fact, a boring night sounds a little too good to me right now. All I really want is an adult beverage, to plop in front of the TV and zone out for a little while."

"All of those things can be arranged." He wanted to be able to give her a break. "Nothing has been going on at your place so far. I'm hoping it stays that way, but one of my guys will be looking out either way."

"Your daughter seems like a really sweet person, by the way," she said. Those words pierced him in the chest as he navigated onto I-30, heading toward Arlington.

"She's a handful most of the time," he said with a head shake and a smile. "But, yeah, she's my world."

"You're doing a great job with her, Rory."

"I hope so," he admitted. "Mind if I ask a question?"

"Go for it," she said.

"How much am I about to rock her world with the bomb I'm going to drop on her?" he asked. "Tell me straight."

"It'll be a shock at first, for sure," she said. "At her age, though, she'll adapt pretty easily. Plus, she's gaining the most incredible people in the world. I think once the dust settles, having all these extra people who love her and want to be in her life will make her feel that much more secure." She paused for a beat. "Any girl should be so lucky as to be a Hayes and surrounded by so much love."

"Your honesty means a lot," he admitted. "Can I ask something more personal?"

"Shoot."

"What about meeting a mother?" he asked. "I realize this is something you're facing now, but have you thought about what you would say? How you would react?"

"When I was little, I used to dream about her suddenly showing up at something important like my birthday," she said. "There was always some grand reason why she'd been kept away from me. In my mind, it was all just a big misunderstanding and she wasn't really gone. My father told me she died when

I was too young to remember her. He kept a picture of her on my dresser, but the woman in the picture wasn't even my mother."

"On some level, I understand lying to protect your feelings," he said.

"What do you tell Liv about her mother?" she asked.

"That she had to go away," he said honestly. "I couldn't think up a great reason, so I just told her that her mother had to leave. When she was little, I'm embarrassed to say that I let her believe Leah might come back. I wanted that door to be open. Plus, I was trying to convince myself too. It just never resonated with me that her mother wouldn't want to see her again. I was a hundred percent sure Leah would turn up. She never has and it's been almost thirteen years."

"Has she ever tried to make contact in any way? Send a birthday card?" she asked.

"No, but we moved out of the apartment I'd shared with Leah by the time Liv turned two," he said. "I had enough money to move us into a slightly nicer place at that point. Since my work is separate from my life, I kept my address private."

"With the internet, she could have found you," Emerson pointed out with compassion in her voice.

"I know," he said quietly. "Leah probably wouldn't be that difficult to find if I put a little effort into it."

"What's stopping you?" Emerson asked.

"Stubbornness," he said on a chuckle. "I keep

thinking that if she wants to see Liv, she should be the one to ask."

"Maybe track her down for Liv," Emerson said. "I've always been curious about my mother even though I got the sense talking about her made my dad sad. The thought of finding this one who I didn't even know about scares me to death. What if she doesn't want to meet me? What if she doesn't care? I ask myself if I can handle the rejection."

"What's keeping you going?" he asked.

"Because I have to know," she said on a shrug. "It's as simple and as complicated as that."

Chapter Fifteen

Emerson couldn't explain why she felt the need to see a woman who might slam the door in her face. "If I don't get my questions answered, I'll regret it later. People only get so much time on this earth and hers might already be up for all I know. It's the questions that would keep me up at night. Ever since finding out the person in the frame on my dresser was a decoy, I've had some sleepless nights. I was already on vacation from work, so I decided to do some digging. I knew I couldn't let this go without answers."

"What if you find her and she doesn't care?" he asked. "Would it be better not to know than to face rejection?"

"I've thought about that a lot," she admitted. "Obviously, that's not how I want this to go. But how will I know if I don't go there? Right?"

"You make a valid point," he said, and she could tell he was asking for Liv. The fact he trusted Emerson's judgment meant more than she could express.

"Liv has the buffer of you," she pointed out. "If

Leah truly doesn't want to see her daughter again or ever talk to her, that's something you can find out before you bring Liv into the picture. But at least you'll know."

"Part of me thinks Leah doesn't deserve a second chance," he said. "I'm not proud of it, but it's true."

"Everyone does," Emerson gently pointed out. "Like you said earlier, everyone makes mistakes. Clearly, some are bigger than others but none of us are perfect."

Those words seemed to resonate with him.

"If you want, I'll go with you when you track her down. I'll knock on that door right beside you," she continued. "Liv is going to want to know about her mother. She might not openly question you now, but that doesn't mean Leah isn't on Liv's mind."

"I guess I hadn't thought about it in that way," he admitted. "Liv is so into her own world that I wasn't sure if her mother ever crossed her mind anymore."

"She does," Emerson stated. "Trust me."

Rory drew in a deep breath before nodding. "One step at a time. First, we focus on your situation. I'd like to introduce Liv to my side of the family and give her a chance to settle before I go tracking down Leah. I can only imagine what she's doing and where she is at this point."

"If you take one piece of advice from me, hear me out on this." She figured she might as well go for broke. "Don't wait too long. Because the waiting is awful when you get to be my age."

Rory reached for her hand, and then gave it a squeeze as he one-handed the steering wheel.

"I won't," he promised. "Not after realizing the kind of pain you're going through."

"Good," she said. "I can't guarantee everything will be smooth or that Leah will welcome Liv into her life. But this will answer so many questions for Liv. And she's not even aware of some of them yet. Or maybe she is. I only just met her, so clearly I don't know her. And yet I got the impression she was a very sensitive and caring person. I doubt she would ever bring up her mother for fear it might hurt your feelings in some way."

"It wouldn't," he said. "I want Liv to talk to me about the hard stuff."

"Don't take this the wrong way, but you were eighteen when you had her and you couldn't talk to your mother about the hard stuff," she said, figuring she might as well lay the cards on the table. They were being honest and this was as truthful as it got.

"Damn," he said. "You're right. I had a hard-as-hell time talking to her now and I'm a grown man."

"No one wants to disappoint a loved one," she said. Her father had banked on the sentiment. She'd kept all her questions quiet, and he'd let her. "Trust me when I say that Liv will appreciate you being the one to bring these things up."

"You really think so?" he asked.

"I'm one hundred percent certain," she confirmed. "There's no easy way to go about it but once you get the dialogue started, she might surprise you with her maturity."

"One minute she's like talking to a grown adult and the next…eye rolling," he said with a warm smile.

"That pretty much describes every teenager, I'm pretty certain," she said on a laugh as he turned into her neighborhood. A random thought struck. "This is a complete change in subject, but do you think the fire today is connected to you helping me? If someone figured out who you were, they would easily be able to find your construction company name."

Rory seemed to consider the idea for a long moment.

"Cecile said the fire marshal claimed it could be arson," he said. "So, anything is possible. There was a smaller fire before we connected, though."

"Whoever is behind this might have been trying to get you out of town and away from the investigation," she pointed out.

"Well, they're about to get a big surprise when I'm back at it tomorrow morning," he said.

"Are you concerned about Liv?" she asked.

"My home address is private and secure," he stated. "She'll be fine with Cecile there."

"It's your crew that has been watching my house today," she said. "I'm also wondering if whoever was behind the fire was trying to draw attention to the Dallas site and maybe leave my home vulnerable."

"There's something in there they want," he reasoned.

"Everything happens on computers these days," she said. "Couldn't they just wipe a hard drive by using a tech guru?"

"It would be possible to do that from a distance," he said as he slowed his speed. "But then some things are still on paper because plenty of folks don't trust computers where I'm from."

Could there be some sort of paper trail?

RORY PARKED IN front of Emerson's one-story brick home, blocking the driveway leading to a two-car garage. "Let me text Mario to let him know it's us." She'd given him the code to get through the garage, so he was able to check out the inside and wait there.

"It'll be good to go inside and pack up a few things now that my overnight bag was stolen," she said as he fired off a text.

Lights were on inside the house, and the glow from a TV was visible through the picture window. A few seconds after the message was sent, a shadow passed by the window. The door opened, and Mario filled the frame.

"Looks good," Rory said to Emerson as he cut the engine and exited the driver's side. This time, she waited the couple of seconds for him to round the front of his truck to open the door for her.

After thanking him, she led the way. Mario immediately introduced himself and then apologized for the mess he'd made. Walking into the front room, Rory immediately saw what his crew member was talking about. The smell of stale pizza hit as he'd stepped into the entryway. An opened, empty box of pizza sat on the coffee table, which was covered in crushed up-napkins and empty soda cans. There were a few taco wrappers in the mix.

"How long have you been here?" Rory asked.

"Couple of hours," Mario said with a shrug. "Why?"

"No reason," Rory said, cracking a smile.

Mario had missed his calling. The oversize, stubborn man should be on the defensive line for the Dallas Cowboys. He liked to eat and play video games when he was off the clock.

"Thank you for giving up your evening to keep watch over this place," Emerson said with a warm smile.

Mario swatted an invisible fly as he made a phsh noise. "Weren't no trouble at all."

"I got it from here, man," Rory said. "Thanks again. I appreciate it."

"Anything for you," Mario said, raking a hand through his dark curls. "You know that."

"Same here," Rory said as Mario started to clean up.

"I got this," Rory said. "Don't even worry about it."

After a brief goodbye, Mario was out the door, and Emerson wasted no time locking it behind him.

"Think we'll be okay here?" she asked after returning from the kitchen with a garbage bag.

"My guys will be in and around, just not inside the house," he said, hoping to ease at least some of her fears. At some point soon, they would sleep and he'd already decided to keep eyes on the home since that would leave them vulnerable.

"I have an alarm but got complacent about arming it," she said. "I'm not even sure I paid the permit fee to the city, so that probably lapsed."

"We can arm it anyway. The alarm company should still respond, and they'll call Arlington police. At the worst, you'll pay a fine for not having a permit," he said.

"Good to know and that would be a small price to pay if we needed to use it," she stated as she opened the garbage bag and leaned over to pick up trash.

"Why don't you go take that shower you've been thinking about while I take care of this," he said.

"Are you sure?" she asked.

"One hundred percent," he confirmed. "I'm guessing trash is out front."

"The brown bin is for trash and green is for recycle," she noted. "Oh, and they're both inside the garage against the wall."

"Got it," he said.

She started for the hallway and then stopped. "Thanks for everything you're doing and everything you've done. I hope I'm half as good a friend to you as you are to me."

The word *friend* shouldn't feel like being impaled right through the heart like it did. He forced himself to find a smile before responding.

"You are," he confirmed. The insight she'd shared about Liv needing to find her mother, and how his daughter was feeling, was worth any sacrifice. But then, it wasn't a hardship to be with Emerson.

She disappeared down the hallway, so he refocused on cleaning up Mario's mess. It didn't take long considering he already had a garbage bag in hand. Emerson's place was small but cozy. The entryway opened up to a living area, which in turn led to a dining room and kitchen. There was a small hall closet next to the front door. Since the garage was in front, the backyard wasn't as well lit. An intruder could enter through the back of the house if she didn't think to turn on the back porch light.

He checked windows and door locks. He would never understand the trend to use so much glass in or around a door. The locks were the twist kind too, which made it that much easier to punch through the glass and unlock.

Even though all the windows he'd checked so far were locked, they didn't offer much in the way of stopping a determined criminal. The alarm would be a big help and give him a heads-up if a door opened. He needed to ask if she'd extended the coverage to windows as well.

The door to the garage could be found through the first right at the mouth of the hallway. There was a tiled laundry room he had to pass through to get to the door leading to the garage. He left the door open as he tied off the trash bag. There were two stalls with enough light from outside to navigate the carless room. Her Bronco was still with Jimmy. Rory wondered if he should think about having it transferred to a local shop rather than keeping it in Cider Creek. He didn't like the break-in one bit or the fact someone had not only her home address but also her overnight bag. She'd said there wasn't much inside other than a bag full of toiletries and enough clothing to get through a couple of nights. Still, the thought of someone going through her personal things ate at him.

Halfway across the garage, he heard footsteps on the other side. A shadow moved across the square window. He fished out his cell phone and sent Mario a text.

U still here?

The response came back a second later.

No.

Well, it couldn't possibly be him. Then who? Rory set the bag down and doubled back into the entryway. Going out the front door would alert the person on the other side to Rory's presence.

Heading to a window was no good. With the lights on in the living room, he'd been seen. At least if he went out the front, he could surprise whoever was out there. Maybe even recognize them. It was worth a shot.

He gripped the door handle and quietly twisted the lock mechanism. In one swift movement, he swung the door open and burst outside. He surveyed the area but didn't see anyone. The light over the garage covered only a small spot.

And then he heard footsteps and a grunt. Someone had just taken off and hopped a fence. Rory cursed underneath his breath. There was no way he could go after the person and leave Emerson vulnerable. At the very least, someone was snooping around. Casing the place?

He closed and locked the door behind him as he walked back in the house and then finished tossing the garbage bag into the bin. By the time he made it back to the living room, Emerson was out of the shower and dressed in yoga pants and a T-shirt that clung to sexy curves. Her hair was slicked back in a low ponytail and droplets of water slid down her neck. He flexed and released his fingers a couple of times to work out some of the sudden tension.

"Somebody was here," he said to her.

"Right now?" she asked, eyes wide.

He nodded, hating to give her the news. "I scared them away, most likely for the night and as long as my truck is parked out front."

"Speaking of which, what time tomorrow do you want to head back to Cider Creek?" she asked.

"Early," he said. "I'd like to beat the traffic, if possible."

"I can be up by around six o'clock," she said. "Is that good?"

"That works," he said. "Since the perp is gone, it might be a good time for me to grab a shower."

"Go right ahead," she said. "All I want is a little Netflix and a glass of wine."

Rory jogged out to his truck to retrieve his backpack. He kept it filled with supplies in case he got called out of town on a job as his business had been expanding all over Texas in recent years. He never knew when he might have to hit the road. He also kept a shotgun in a special holder underneath the seat. He retrieved it too.

Before reentering the house, he took another look around.

Chapter Sixteen

Emerson needed a few minutes to clear her mind, and the best way to do that was to watch something funny. She put on a comedy special, paused it and then poured herself a glass of wine. By the time she settled down on the couch, Rory came back inside. The shotgun tucked underneath his shoulder was a reminder of how seriously they needed to take the situation.

"Do you know how to use one of these?" he asked, motioning toward the weapon.

"I've been to the range a few times," she said. "My father used to take me." She was beginning to wonder if he'd expected someone to come after them someday. *After her?*

"Good," he said. "I'll leave this with you while I grab a shower."

She nodded. "There's beer in the fridge if you're thirsty."

"I'll take you up on that after my shower," he said.

"Guest bath is the second door on your right." She motioned toward the hallway and tried to force thoughts of him naked out of her brain. She hit Play on the remote, and the comedian's voice helped distract her. She turned down the volume, in case someone was outside.

Laughing might be too much to hope for, but a couple of jokes in, the comedian put a smile on her face. It helped lighten her mood. Tucking her feet underneath her bottom, she hugged a throw pillow and sipped on wine.

Rory was out of the shower and in a heartbeat was in fresh jeans that hung low on his hips. The vision of his muscled chest with literal ripples wasn't something she could afford to focus on. She sat up a little straighter as he moved to the kitchen, and then came back with an opened beer bottle. He took a seat at the far end of the couch as the room suddenly crackled with tension. She turned up the volume a notch, like that would help. Not even a bucket of ice water could cool the temperature.

Emerson took in a couple of deep breaths. The last person who'd used her shower had been Timothy Wrath. Her last relationship had been a year and a half ago. Really? She rechecked her math. That was right. A full eighteen months had passed since Timothy. Their relationship had been short-lived. He'd accused her of starting to pull back almost the moment things got serious. She'd watched him spend a whole lot of time on his cell phone, texting with a coworker during their "binge" nights on the couch. Timothy's relationship status changed two weeks after the breakup. She wasn't surprised his new profile picture was him with said coworker. They were all smiles and, after the sting of jealousy subsided, she was happy for them both.

Besides, she wasn't then and most likely never would be ready for marriage and kids. An image of her, Rory and Liv as a family popped into Emerson's thoughts, surprising her.

The comedian must have told a good joke because a low rumble of a laugh came out from deep in Rory's chest. A voice shouldn't travel all over someone like his had a way of doing. At least she was able to force the family image of them out of her mind. Liv was a sweet girl, but Emerson wasn't the mothering type. That kid deserved the world. She'd already hit it out of the park when it came to one parent. Rory's attentiveness to Liv was above and beyond. She could tell how torn he was about making the right move when it came to telling Liv about the family she didn't know she had and the mother who'd walked out of her life.

The show ended around the same time she finished her glass of wine. It was just what she needed to relax before bedtime. She noticed Rory had only finished half of his beer before setting the glass bottle on top of a coaster, where it had stayed during the comedy special.

"Ready for bed?" she asked after clicking off the TV using the remote. She also heard how that sounded. "What I meant to say was ready to go to your bed? In the guest room?"

She'd already asked him to sleep with her for one night. A second night in a row was probably asking too much, and she didn't want to put him in an awkward spot where he felt like he had to agree.

"Will you be all right?" he asked.

"I'll probably leave the door open, just in case."

"I can sleep with you if it'll help you rest better," he continued like it was the most normal thing. Just the thought of being in bed with him, here in her own home, was enough to release a half dozen butterflies in her stomach. "It's no trouble."

"You didn't get much rest last night, if memory serves," she said. "You ended up conking out on a chair. Your neck is probably still stiff."

"That's fair," he said with a dry crack of a smile. He was a little too good at releasing those butterflies with a look or the way his voice wrapped around her like a caress. "What if I promise to stay in bed all night then?"

"I'd have to say it would be a shame we were only sleeping," she quipped, thinking the comment would be funny if there wasn't so much truth to it.

He cleared his throat, and then laughed.

"Either way, I'm here in case you need me," he said. "Can't say that I've slept in a whole lot of guest rooms but there's a first for everything."

Before she could pick her jaw up off the floor, he laughed again, and she realized he was just kidding. The break in tension was a welcome change.

"If we keep these rolling, think we'll get our own

comedy show?" she asked, returning her wineglass to the kitchen counter. He poured the rest of his beer down the sink and then tossed the bottle in the recycle bin underneath.

"They're probably trying to call right now and we're just not picking up," he said, keeping the line going.

"In all seriousness, I should be fine," she said. "I wasn't kidding about leaving the door open, though, and I hope you'll leave yours the same just in case."

"You can bet on it," he said. "I'm a light sleeper anyway, so I'll wake up at the slightest noise."

She nodded, thinking that was good because she was just the opposite. "Once I'm asleep, a freight train could roll through the room and I probably wouldn't hear it."

"Good, then you won't mind my snoring." He cracked another one of those devastating smiles that released more butterflies. Then he relaxed and reached for her hand. "In all seriousness, I've been thinking about the advice you gave in the truck on the way over. It struck me a little hard, which means you hit on something I needed to hear. Anyway, I just wanted to say thanks again for your honesty."

Standing there with only a couple of feet between them, his hand around hers, her pulse thundered. She had to fight every urge to take a step toward him and kiss this gorgeous man in her kitchen.

"You're welcome," she said to him. There was something stirring behind his eyes. Was it desire?

Did he feel the same pull toward her? Did it matter? He admitted that he didn't have time for anything besides his daughter and his career. Now that he'd come clean with his mother about Liv, he was about to have a whole bunch of family in his life. Even if their attraction was mutual, where could it really go?

Emerson would laugh if that was funny. Instead, she tried not to let the reality sink in too harshly. A relationship with Rory Hayes would be a blazing fire. She could only imagine how incredible the sex would be based on the heat in the few kisses they'd shared. They'd practically melted her. She could still taste dark-roast coffee from his lips. Coffee had never tasted so good.

And since it was taking all the willpower she could muster not to lean into him and let this raging wildfire burn, she dropped his hand and took a step back.

"Sleep tight," was all she could think to say before backing out of the room altogether before she did something she might regret, like ask Rory to come to bed with her.

RORY'S FINGERTIPS SIZZLED from the fiery flame that was Emerson. He'd been so close to asking her if he could kiss her that he had to clench his back teeth to stop the words from coming out. It had been a long time since he'd been able to really talk to someone about Liv. In fact, he couldn't remember the last time he'd confided in someone or solicited advice. Cecile was great, but she was the first to say how skilled she was in business. She drove a sports car for a reason: no room for a car seat in back. In her early fifties, she claimed to be too old to be a mother but she'd taken Liv under her wing. He'd been grateful to have a mother figure at all in Liv's life.

Emerson's concern for whether or not Liv had had dinner and whether or not she liked milkshakes had touched him in a place long forgotten. This was what he thought he'd had with Leah when he was too young to know the difference between infatuation and real love. Real love was something that lasted. It endured, even when times got tough. He'd witnessed it firsthand with his parents and he knew his mother had stayed on at the ranch with her difficult father-in-law because she felt closer to her husband there. She had no inkling to date in the decade and a half since losing her husband. She'd told Rory that she would always be married to his father, and once she'd had the best, there was no reason to go looking for anyone else.

He was beginning to understand a love like theirs. Even at eighteen, he knew his relationship with Leah wasn't built to last. He'd naively believed their feelings would grow deeper over the years. They'd rushed to the altar because he'd needed to do the right thing by her. There was no way he would let her go through a pregnancy by herself, without him beside her. He'd believed it was the two of them against the world, and that together they would figure it all out. *A weak foundation can't hold a whole lot of weight.*

Rory might have learned the lesson the hard way but he wouldn't trade Liv for the world. On that note, he decided it was time for bed. The whole melancholy mood he was grasping was the last thing he needed.

After brushing his teeth, he slid out of his clean jeans and underneath the covers in the guest room. A plug-in light from the hallway provided enough illumination to avoid tripping over a piece of furniture if he needed to get up and out of the room quickly. He'd placed his shotgun next to the bed, just in case.

Tonight, he fell asleep thinking about Emerson's advice about finding Leah and the effect the reunion might have on Liv. If he could protect that kid from the world, he would do it in a heartbeat. If he could feel all her pain instead of helplessly standing by and watching his sweet girl ache, he would trade places without question. The hardest thing about parenting wasn't all the years of diaper changes and late-night feedings. It was watching his kid suffer in any way. That was the worst. He'd heard people describe having children as watching their hearts walk around outside their bodies, and he couldn't agree more.

Liv was his heart. Was there room for anyone else? Someone like Emerson? He was beginning to think it might be a possibility, and his heart sped up at the thought.

Right now, the best he could do for her was help

her find answers and figure out who was trying to stop her.

Rory's thoughts drifted to the construction site fire. Thankfully, no one was injured. Was it meant to be a warning? Was someone trying to get his attention? Or take it away from this case?

Either way, Rory wasn't walking away until they had answers. And he needed to circle back to Bynum Ross to ask a few questions no matter how defiant and dismissive the old man had been.

Rory woke the next morning with those same thoughts on his mind. There was no sun this morning as he glanced at the clock, which read six-twenty. He'd overslept. Liv would be up and getting ready for school. She had another week and a half before Thanksgiving break started. The first text of the day was from his mother, asking if he had plans.

Thanksgiving at Hayes Cattle?

The old saying "one can never truly go home" came to mind. Was it true? Now that he'd cleared the air with his mother, he found that he actually wanted to show Liv around the ranch. He wanted her to experience riding horses and herding cattle. He couldn't ignore the fact ranching was in her blood too. And maybe he would consider getting her that hairless cat after all.

Leah might surprise him even though evidence didn't suggest it. He would try to keep an open mind without forgetting the past and what she put him through. Liv deserved better but she also deserved to know if her mother wanted to be in her life.

He could see that so clearly now that he'd spent time with Emerson. It was obvious how important the relationship, the answers might be to Liv. He'd been coasting with her, figuring the conversation wouldn't come up and that she was over it. Now he could see how foolish he'd been. The subject was uncomfortable for him and he'd dropped the ball. It became so easy to let it ride and hope for the best. His approach was the equivalent of sticking his head in the sand. He could see that so clearly in the hurt in Emerson's eyes when she talked about her own father withholding information about her mother.

Granted, this wasn't exactly an apples-to-apples comparison. They didn't know what they were dealing with in her mother's case.

His cell phone buzzed as he threw on a pair of jeans. He checked the screen. It was his mother calling.

"Hello," he answered.

"You mentioned something yesterday about your friend's situation while she was outside," his mother started right in. When she got something stuck in her craw, there was no stopping her until she sorted it all out.

"I told you about the chilly reception she received from Bynum Ross," he stated.

"And then about her vehicle being broken into right before she came over," his mother said. "I couldn't sleep when you told me that because I was almost one hundred percent certain your grandfather and Bynum were in cahoots with each other," she said. "I logged on to his computer and found a few emails with them talking about the possibility of something resurfacing and how they should handle it. I've been sifting through his emails until my eyes are blurry and I should probably get some sleep. I just remember overhearing a few conversations between Duncan and Bynum that had made me feel like they were hiding something. At the time, I blew it off. We've never had much in the way of a conspiracy around here. But the way they had spoken in hushed whispers had always made me think they were hiding something."

"Thanks for the call," he said to his mom. "We're about to head that way after breakfast. You should know that one of my construction sites burned down. Another had a small fire. The arson investigator believes it could be deliberate and that makes me think it's a little too much of a coincidence that since I started helping Emerson another one of my construction sites is lit on fire."

"Doesn't sound like a random occurrence," his mother said. He was grateful she felt she could reach out to him whenever she had an idea. This was new territory in their relationship, but he liked the direction it was going. "Are you in danger?"

"I can handle whatever comes my way," he replied.

"What about Liv?" she immediately asked. "Could they do anything to her?"

"No one should have a problem with my daughter, but if they come for her, they better be ready to face me," he said The thought anyone could come for Liv burned him to no end.

"She's welcome to stay here at the ranch, along with Emerson, of course," his mother said.

"I might just take you up on that." He figured the surest way to keep everyone safe was to keep them together at the ranch.

"Thanksgiving break is almost here," his mother continued. "I bet Liv could finish out her schoolwork online."

"It's possible," he said. Then, he paused for a long moment. "I haven't even tried to contact Leah since she walked out. I'm guessing you haven't heard anything about her or her family."

"Not since they moved away, no," she said. "They didn't keep in touch, but then we weren't as close as the two of you were."

A moment of silence sat between them.

"I'm sorry for how everything turned out with Leah," his mom said. "It sounds like she abandoned you when you needed her the most. There's no excuse for that in a relationship and that must have made it difficult to trust anyone else."

"There hasn't been a whole lot of time for anyone else," he said a little too quickly. "All I mean is that I've had my hands full between running a business and bringing up my daughter. I wouldn't trade either one."

"I'm proud of the success you've become," his mom said. There was something about hearing those words from her that brought more comfort than he could ever have imagined. "And you're doing an amazing job with your daughter."

"How can you tell?" he asked.

"Because you care so much," she insisted. "It shows in how you talk about her and how much you love her. I'm sorry you didn't feel like you could come to me. But, you're doing an amazing job on your own."

"You know that saying it takes a village?" he asked.

"Yes."

"I'm ready for the village to step in," he said. "I've done the best I could so far, but there's always room for improvement, and there's no such thing as too much love. I just want her to be happy and safe."

"Sounds like good parenting to me," his mom said. "And, son, the village is ready anytime you are."

"Good," he said. "Because you have been an amazing mom and I can't think of a better role model for Liv."

"I'd say she has a couple of positive women entering her life," his mom said in true cryptic fashion. He could see right through it. She was talking about Emerson, and he had no idea if she would stick around once she found her own mother and settled back into her life here in Arlington. She'd made a good life for herself and he had no idea if there was room for anyone else.

A growing part of him wanted to find out, though.

Chapter Seventeen

"Morning."

That one word shouldn't make Emerson's heart sing the way it did when spoken by Rory. She smiled and handed over a cup of coffee. Focusing on her situation rather than giving in and letting her gaze roam his chest, she cleared her throat to clear the air.

"Last night was quiet," she pointed out. She'd gotten a good night of sleep, and that always worked wonders for her stress levels and mood.

"That it was," he said, taking the offering.

"I'm not much of a cook but I managed toast and scrambled eggs." A fancy meal for her when she normally just ate a piece of fruit and yogurt or a breakfast bar. She set the plate down on the counter and then located a fork. "Dig in."

"Looks good," he said with a deep timbre that sounded like pure sin. No one person should get have much sex appeal. Be still her heart.

Aside from an overload of sexiness, he was also kind and compassionate, traits she valued more than

anything else. There was something about personality and magnetism that could make a person more
or less attractive. In his case, it worked to the positive in spades.

He finished off the food on the plate in a matter
of a minute, and then rinsed it off before placing it
inside the dishwasher. His coffee cup was drained
another minute later.

"Are you ready to get on the road?" he asked.
They had a five-hour drive in front of them, and he
seemed eager to get going. Since they could continue
their discussion on the road, she agreed.

"I can be out the door in five minutes," she said
before exiting the room. It was more like four minutes, twenty seconds by the time she stood at the
front door, bag in hand. She had to use her gym
bag since her overnight bag had been stolen from
her Bronco. Speaking of which, she needed to text
Jimmy for an update.

She set the alarm and then headed out the door
first, locking it behind Rory. After placing their bags
in the back seat, she climbed into the passenger seat
and scanned the area. The thought someone might
be out there, lurking, waiting for her to leave so they
could ransack her home as well gave her an uneasy
feeling.

"All I did was go to Cider Creek to ask about a
woman in a picture," she said. "How on earth did
that stir up this much trouble?"

"I've been thinking about that too," he said. "My

mom called this morning and she remembers over-hearing hushed conversations between my grandfa-ther and Bynum Ross. Since my grandfather is gone, the only person we can talk to is Bynum. Are you okay with going back to B-T?"

"Whatever it takes to get answers," she said, al-though she wasn't looking forward to seeing Bynum again or walking into B-T. At least she had the power of the Hayes family behind her now. The name got people's attention and might buy her a lot of cred-ibility.

"He'll be our first stop," Rory said emphatically.

"What did your mother overhear?" she asked.

"Nothing concrete," he admitted. "It's one of those 'where there's smoke, there's fire' situations. At least, that's the thinking. Their conversations might not have anything to do with what's happening with you, but we won't know until we do a little digging. I'm sure my mom is in her father-in-law's office and on the computer doing a little research of her own."

"I have to hope that if we keep at it, something will turn up," she said.

"You mentioned your aunt before," he said. "What about her? Think we could swing by on our way out of town and ask her a few questions?"

"Why not?" She fished out her cell phone and pulled up her aunt's contact, tapping the name to initiate a call.

"Hello?" The fact Emerson's name came up on the screen didn't seem to register with her aunt. She answered like the caller was a surprise to her every time. At least she was consistent and gave Emerson a reason to smile.

"Hi, Aunt Ginny."

"Oh, hello," Aunt Ginny said. It was highly possible her aunt had never added Emerson as a contact. She would be the first to admit she didn't care a hill of beans about technology.

"Is this a good time?" Emerson asked.

"I can pause my show."

"Could I stop by?"

"Well, sure, honey," Aunt Ginny said. Of all the years Emerson had lived near her aunt, the two had never formed a close bond. Aunt Ginny was still of the mindset children should be seen and not heard, so the two had rarely ever held a conversation. By the time Emerson was old enough to speak, in Aunt Ginny's mind, she'd lost interest.

"How about in—" Emerson glanced at the clock on the dashboard "—ten minutes?"

"Right now's good," Aunt Ginny said. "Is there a reason for the visit?"

"I'm on my way out of town and I just wanted to stop by first." It was an honest answer without going into detail.

"Well, then, I'll see you in a few minutes," Aunt Ginny said, sounding more than a little caught off guard by the unexpected phone call and plan to visit.

After saying their goodbyes and hanging up, Emerson plugged the address into her phone's GPS to guide Rory. She set it down in the cup holder in between them so she wouldn't have to hold on to it. The directions would be spoken out loud, so she didn't need to worry about watching a screen. Plus, her aunt's place wasn't far.

"I could have asked questions on the phone, but I figured it would be best if we stopped by in person," she explained. "That way, we can gauge her reactions to my questions. I highly doubt she'll be honest with me after brushing me off before. But maybe we can get a little more out of her while making eye contact." That was the hope at least. Even though she'd never been close to Aunt Ginny, the woman was a terrible liar. Emerson had read it so clearly in Aunt Ginny's eyes after confronting her.

"Good call," he said. His grip on the steering wheel was so tight his knuckles turned white.

"Everything okay this morning?" she asked.

"I never realized my grandfather was this close to Bynum Ross," he said after clenching his back teeth. "The man didn't exactly have friends to my knowledge, and I can't imagine much changed after I left town. Strange how you can think you know someone and then find out they have secrets."

"Agreed," she said, feeling every inch of those words in her soul. "He was a jerk to you and it wasn't fair."

"You'd think I'd want to blame him for what happened," he said. "He's at fault, but so am I."

"You were young," she countered, hating that he was blaming himself for a grown man's actions who took advantage of Rory's inexperience and youth.

"What about Leah?" he asked. "Shouldn't I have known something was wrong? Shouldn't I have clued in when she was so tired all she wanted to do was sleep?"

"Once again, you were young and it was probably your first serious relationship," she pointed out. "I'm not absolving you from all responsibility. All I'm saying is that you have to give yourself a little grace there. If you were repeating those mistakes, not learning from them, then I'd be worried. Sounds to me like you've been beating yourself up for years over actions that came about when you were barely old enough shave."

He stared out the front windshield, squinting against the blaring sun.

"When you put it like that, it does sound as if I'm going a little overboard," he said. "Guess I should stop being so hard on myself for the past."

"I think that's a lesson everyone needs to learn," she said. "You're not alone in that one, and it's so much easier to see someone else's mistakes than your own. Ever notice that?"

"Honestly? I'm so knee-deep into my work and not messing up raising a daughter that I don't have time for much else," he said with a raw honesty that touched her soul.

"Burying yourself in work is a sure way not to have to deal with anyone or anything else," she said.

"When you put it like that, it sounds like avoidance," he reasoned.

"Isn't it?"

After a thoughtful pause, he nodded.

"I had to in the early days after Leah left," he admitted. "Then it just became easier to shrink my life to work and Liv."

"You're an amazing dad," she said to him. "Liv is an incredible kid and you did that all by yourself. You have a lot to be proud of with her."

RORY WASN'T CERTAIN why hearing those words from Emerson meant so much, but it did.

"You're pretty special too," he said. "For all your father's mistakes, and it sounds like there were plenty, you turned out to be an incredible woman."

From the driver's seat, he could almost feel her blushing. She needed to hear those words, though. She was right. Looking in from the outside always gave him a better perspective. Facing Leah was something he needed to do for himself as much as for Liv. He saw that clearly now. He would never be able to let go of the past without knowing she was all right and saying his piece to her about the damage he might be doing to their daughter.

"I don't know about that, but thank you anyway,"

Emerson said so quietly he almost didn't hear her.
She was a beautiful person inside and out, and she
needed to know how special she was.

GPS interrupted the moment, telling him to turn
right at the next light. He did. Two lights later, and
he was pulling up to a bungalow with metal fencing
in the front yard. He pulled up to house number 223,
as instructed by the phone.

"You're coming inside with me, right?" she asked.

He cut off the engine.

"It might help to have an objective observer in
the room," he said.

"Good." She took in a slow, deep breath.

"Plus, I'd just like to be there for you as much as
you'll let me," he stated, feeling raw like he'd just
opened a vein. The admission made him realize he
never let anyone get close to him anymore other than
Liv. And he had secrets from her that he had no idea
how she would react to. Tension coiled in his chest
thinking about the heartache that kid might have
coming, but he was realizing it was important to go
through the steps. Let her get it out of her system and
move on. At the very least, he hoped her questions
about her mother would be answered.

Clean slate.

He exited the truck and came around to the passenger side as Emerson slipped out. She stopped, and
he could see the hesitation in her eyes. She gripped
his forearms and leaned against the opened door.

"You got this," he said to her. Then, without debating his next actions, he did the most natural thing and kissed her. The second his lips pressed to hers, a fireworks show went off inside him. There was no way he would risk deepening the kiss, especially here in front of her aunt's home, but he reasoned it was probably best if her relative believed they were a couple.

Emerson brought her hands up to his chest and there were more fireworks. It would be a little too easy to get lost with her, so he pulled back and pressed his forehead against hers to give them both a minute to catch their breath.

"Thanks for that," Emerson said. "I needed a distraction."

Friend and *distraction* were becoming his least favorite words.

Standing for a few minutes, so close he could breathe in her unique flower-and-citrus scent, was doing nothing to dull his desire—a desire that was a physical force all of its own. Although he could admit to keeping everyone at arm's length since Leah, a draw like the one he felt toward Emerson was new territory for him. He'd never felt anything like it, and something deep, something primal within him said that he never would again.

After a deep inhale and exhale, Emerson straightened her shoulders, looked him in the eye and said, "I'm as ready as I'll ever be."

He reached for her hand and linked their fingers. He was a little taken aback when she withdrew her hand. Since this wasn't the time to ask questions, he filed the information away while trying to recover from the sting of the rejection as best as he could while refocusing on what they needed to get out of her aunt.

Emerson rang the doorbell, and they waited.

There was no answer.

"That's strange," she said. "We were just on the phone."

A noise like a screen door smacking against the wall came from the back of the house.

"Grab the shotgun out of my truck," Rory said as he stuffed his hand inside his pocket and hit the unlock button on the key fob. It was taking a risk going after whoever bolted out the back door. He didn't like leaving Emerson alone, not even with her aunt, in case there was someone else inside the home. He doubted it, but there was no way to be certain. "Be careful."

He shouted the last part as he ran around the side of the home, dogs barking as someone flew past. Rory was a fast runner from playing sports back in the day, but he realized how out of shape he was in when it came to cardio as he rounded the back.

Visibility wasn't a problem with all the chain-link fencing. He caught a glimpse of someone as he disappeared in between a pair of houses several homes down the block. It would be too easy for the guy to circle back if Rory gave chase. And this person was fast, basically a blur. The thought of leaving Emerson alone and vulnerable despite her ability to shoot didn't sit well.

A scream of terror got his feet moving back the way he came.

Chapter Eighteen

Emerson clamped her hand over her mouth to stop herself from screaming again as she ran to her aunt, who was tied to a chair with some kind of thick cord around her neck. Her head was tilted to one side at an awkward angle and her eyes were closed but her chest was moving up and down.

"Aunt Ginny," Emerson managed to get out as she cut across the kitchen floor of the home, which looked like a relic left over from the seventies with vinyl flooring and a retro table-and-chair set tucked in the corner.

Emerson loosened the noose around her aunt's neck, praying now that Aunt Ginny was getting oxygen to her brain so that she would wake up. "Aunt Ginny, it's me."

Tears welled in Emerson's eyes as she reached for her aunt's wrist to check for a pulse. As her fingers closed around her aunt's thick arm, her eyes blinked open and she gasped. Her hands came up to her neck as she felt around the red marks and indentation.

"I'm here, Aunt Ginny," Emerson said. "You're okay."

At that moment, the back door burst open. Emerson whipped around and aimed the shotgun at the door before it registered that it was Rory. He put his hands in the air.

"Don't shoot," he said, his gaze shifting from Emerson to her aunt and back again. "I'll call 911."

Emerson nodded before turning back around to her aunt, who must have passed out from the stress or lack of oxygen. "Can you tell me who did this to you?"

"Water," her aunt whispered with a scratchy voice. She winced like it hurt to speak. Emerson worked quickly, remembering the glasses were in the cabinet next to the sink. And then she turned on the spigot to fill the glass.

She needed to know if her aunt recognized the person or persons who did this to her. Handing over the water glass, she repeated her question.

Aunt Ginny took a sip and nodded.

"He said he'd kill you if I ever told," Aunt Ginny managed to get out even though it looked like she had to fight for every word. As much as Emerson wanted to let her aunt rest, the police and an ambulance would be here soon. This might be the only time Emerson had to speak to her to aunt one-on-one.

"Who?" she asked.

"My brother," Aunt Ginny admitted. *Emerson's father?*

"Why?" she pressed, figuring the window of time

was shrinking. Sirens would sound any minute now, and Emerson feared her aunt would shut down altogether.

Her aunt didn't respond. Instead, she offered a helpless look.

"Please, Aunt Ginny," Emerson said as her aunt closed her eyes. "I need your help if I'm going to make sure you're safe. Talk to me." She was almost begging at this point. "Someone broke into your home and did this to you. Help me find out who and bring them to justice."

"M-m-m T-u-r-r-n," was all she said before blinking a few times as though trying to open her eyes but failing. Sirens sounded in the distance, almost on cue and not a minute too late. Her aunt's pulse was still strong but she couldn't seem to keep her eyes open. Emerson cupped her aunt's face in her hands to hold her steady until help arrived.

The next hour and a half was filled with a medical team, statements and crime scene tape. Watching her aunt as she was taken out on a stretcher was one of the worst images, second only to the way she'd found her aunt in the kitchen when she first came through the back door.

When the last police officer left, Emerson found the spare key and locked up. She dropped off her aunt's purse with a neighbor down the street who was her aunt's best friend. Back in the truck and on course, she thought about what her aunt said.

"I couldn't make out what she said before she passed out but I know she's still afraid of my father," Emerson stated. "Which is odd considering the fact he's gone."

"We have no idea how long oxygen had been cut off from her brain before we got there," he pointed out. "The EMT didn't make any promises, but he seemed to feel good about her prognosis."

"The only positive thing to come out of this is that she'll survive." Emerson wanted to know why her aunt was afraid of the man who'd raised her.

"It's possible someone saw the runner," he said.

"Didn't sound like you got much of a look at him." She appreciated Rory circling back to make sure everything was good at her aunt's home, though instead of going after the person who'd taken off. Having Rory there to call 911, be there to offer protection if the guy had returned, and act as a calming presence meant everything.

"Only a glimpse as he turned the corner and he was too far to get any details," he said as he navigated onto the highway, heading south. "The police are involved now and there was an assault on a senior. They'll work hard to catch this guy."

"I just wish we could tie the fire, my crash and this together with something other than loose tethers." The officer had said bad luck seemed to surround her in the past couple of days. She'd told him about searching for her mother, but she could see his dismissal in his eyes. He'd promised to make a note on the case file, but he had about as much enthusiasm as a mother with three rowdy kids watching them drink more Cokes from across the room.

"Any lead would be good," he said with a sharp sigh. "But we're aggravating someone or none of this would be happening."

"All roads lead back to Bynum Ross in my mind," she stated, releasing some of her pent-up frustration by flexing and releasing her fingers. "This all began with him and my guess is that it's going to end with him too."

Rory's cell buzzed, indicating a text had come in.

"Do you mind?" he asked, fishing it out of his pocket and handing it to her. "It might be Liv trying to reach me and this way you can text her back for me."

Emerson checked the screen.

"It's your mother actually," she said, holding up the phone. "She wants you to stop by the house ASAP. Says she found something that might be of interest."

"Are you okay with that? Or do you want to go straight to Bynum's place?" he asked.

"Let's see what your mother found first." She wanted to have as much ammunition as possible to go in with.

"You got it," he said as she settled in for the long drive to Cider Creek, hoping his mother might be able to shed some light on this situation.

RORY MADE THE drive home in record time, stopping only once at a Buc-ee's for food and fuel. The place had just about everything anyone could possibly need, plus the friendliest cashiers. There were enough of them so that he didn't have to wait in a line. Considering his work was expanding around Texas, he'd mapped most of them around the Lone Star State.

He polished off a pair of pulled pork sandwiches, chasing them down with Coke before getting back on the road with a full tank of gas. Emerson had become quiet and he figured she was still shocked about what had happened to her aunt. Running Emerson off the road was one thing, and the fire could have hurt someone, but tying a noose around her aunt's neck and leaving her there meant certain death.

M Turn meant something, but the list of possibilities was too long to venture a real guess. A good starting place might be to assume the *M* stood for Mr. or Mrs. and Turn was the beginning of someone's last name. If not Turn, then a word that sounded like it. A few rhyming words came to mind. Nothing stuck.

The rest of the ride to the ranch was easy, quiet. Both were lost in thought. Every once in a while, she would reach for his arm or he would do the same to her. The occasional touches kept him grounded as he processed the new information.

Before he realized it, he was turning into the drive and up the road to the main house. He parked in the gravel lot next to a vehicle he didn't recognize, looking forward to bringing Liv here someday.

He came around the front of the vehicle after exiting, and then opened the door for Emerson. She slid out and gave him a quick peck on the cheek.

"Thank you," she said softly. "For knowing when I need to talk and when I need to process."

"I can say the same thing to you." There was no other person he'd been so in sync with that just being in her presence made him feel connected. He wasn't one for big conversations or diving deep into subjects, except with her. And he sure didn't take parenting advice from just anyone.

From out of the corner of his eye, he saw a female figure walk out from around the back of the house. She stopped suddenly.

"Rory?"

Her voice was unmistakable. He turned to face her just to make certain his ears weren't playing tricks on him.

"Leah," he said, hearing the mix of surprise and dread in his own voice.

"*The* Leah?" Emerson's eyes widened.

He nodded.

"Go," she urged. "Talk to her."

He reached for Emerson's hand and then linked their fingers. This time, she didn't let go.

"Are you sure you want to do this with me in ear shot?" she asked as they headed toward Leah.

"Wouldn't have it any other way," he said.

"Okay then," she stated. "I'll be right there the whole time."

"I'm counting on it," he said, giving her hand a small squeeze.

Leah shifted her weight from her right foot to her left. She looked the same but much older and he saw a lot of Liv in her. Focusing on that helped a whole lot. He hoped it might carry him through this conversation.

He and Emerson came to a stop a few feet in front of Leah, leaving plenty of room between them. He made introductions and neither offered a handshake.

"What are you doing here?" he asked.

"Granny tracked me down," Leah said, shifting her weight to her other foot. She twisted her arms up and couldn't seem to stand still. She'd always done that when she was nervous. Up close, stress lines marred her forehead and she carried bags underneath her eyes. "I hope it's okay that I asked to come see you."

Was this his mom's big news? Nah, couldn't be. She wouldn't surprise him with Leah. Granny was another story.

"You're here," he said, hearing the defensiveness in his tone.

Emerson glanced up at him and he saw disappointment reflected in her eyes. He bit back a curse, and realized this was his chance to pave the way for

Liv to have a relationship with her mother if Leah was in a good place.

"How are you, Leah?"

She exhaled. If she twisted her fingers any tighter, they might braid permanently.

"I'm good, Rory," she said, shifting her weight for the third time. "I mean, good as I can be. You know?" She held up her left hand and there was a rock on the third finger. "I'm married to a great guy and we live in San Antonio. He's a chef." She dropped her gaze like she was almost ashamed to admit the next part. "We have a little boy. Henry Jack is his name. He's three years old."

He bit back the urge to ask if she was ready for motherhood this time. Berating her for the past wouldn't do any good and he could see how nervous she was. It would be a jerk move to lash out.

And, honestly, he realized how happy he was for Leah. Maybe a little relieved too.

"Sounds like you have it together," he said. "That's good, Leah. I'm proud of you."

"Are you?" she asked with so much hope in her voice that he couldn't be mean.

"Yes. I truly am," he reassured.

"You have no idea what it means for me to hear you say that." She dropped her chin to her chest like she was trying to hide the fact tears were streaming down her cheeks. "The way I left things all those years ago…hiding everything from my family… walking out…it wasn't right."

"Can I ask a question?"

She sniffled and nodded. "Of course. Anything." She tensed up like she was gearing up to take a punch. The move broke his heart. They'd been through enough. The last thing he wanted was for anyone else to suffer anymore.

"Why didn't you try to see her?" he asked.

It was almost as though she couldn't look into his eyes and answer. She literally shuffled her boots like a young one in the playground who was about to get reamed out by the teacher for kicking dirt in someone's face.

"I wanted to," she said, "but figured I'd lost the right a long time ago."

He didn't immediately speak. In part, because she wasn't too off base.

"I can't speak for Liv, but I think it would mean a whole lot to her if she could meet you in person," he said.

The hopeful look on Leah's face when she glanced up at him made him realize he was doing the right thing.

"Do you think so?" she asked. "I wonder what she looks like all the time."

He let go of Emerson's hand long enough to fish out his cell phone.

"Do either of you want a cup of coffee?" Emerson asked.

"No, thank you," Leah said. She held her hand

out. It trembled. "I'd be even worse than this if I had caffeine."

"I'd like one," he said to Emerson. She caught his gaze and held it for a long moment. He got the message.

He nodded before dipping his head to kiss her.

Chapter Nineteen

"How much trouble am I in?" Granny asked the question with a sneaky grin and a wink as Emerson casually walked inside the main house, a house that surprisingly felt a lot like home. It was the warmth, and that had everything to do with the people inside.

Emerson walked over to Granny and gave her a hug.

"You did good," she said.

Granny exhaled like she was releasing a breath she'd been holding. "I was on the internet, and I thought why not try to look her up? All I did was hit a couple of keys." Granny made a show of tapping her fingers on the table as though it was a keyboard. "Poof. There she was. So I DMed her."

"First of all, I'm impressed with your tech savvy," Emerson pointed out. "Plus, you were spot-on with Rory. He needed this more than words can express. You're giving him an amazing gift."

"I thought maybe he might reach out to her now that he's reckoning his past," Granny said after a thoughtful pause. "It was important for me to see what he might be up against."

"Your instincts were right," Emerson reassured.

"Good," Granny said, getting a little choked up on the word. "I was afraid I'd lose him again if I…"

"You never have to worry about that, okay?" Emerson reassured with a big hug. "I may not have known Rory for a very long time but I feel like I know who he is down deep. And he has learned from his mistakes. He keeps beating himself up over allowing his grandfather to push him away all those years ago. He doesn't strike me as the kind of person who makes the same mistake twice."

Granny wiped away a stray tear and sniffled.

"I haven't seen him so comfortable around anyone else but you before," she said. "When he was younger, he didn't open up to a lot of people. I'm guessing that got worse after Leah." She opened her mouth to say something else but seemed to think better of it when she clamped her mouth shut. Instead, she beamed up at Emerson. "Thank you for everything you're doing for him."

"To be honest, I feel like it's the opposite," Emerson said, "but thank you for saying so. It really means a lot."

"How long do you reckon we should give them out there?" Granny asked.

"As much time as they need," Emerson stated as Marla walked into the room.

"I thought I heard voices in here," Marla said.

She glanced out the window. "How's it going with those two?"

"Good, I think," Emerson said. "At least they were on solid footing when I came inside to give them some privacy."

Marla nodded and smiled. It faded quickly when she said, "I have something you're going to want to see. It's about Bynum Ross and my father-in-law."

"Oh, okay," Emerson said, then remembered to ask a question. "Do either of you know of a Mr. or Mrs. Turn-something?"

Both seemed to be searching their memory banks but came up empty.

"Let it sit for a minute," Granny said first. "Maybe something will come up once it percolates for a while."

"In the meantime, follow me," Marla said before walking to an office that was down a long hallway off the kitchen. Again, Emerson was impressed by the size of the place.

The office was the epitome of masculinity. Buck heads hanging on the walls. A massive mahogany desk with an equally grand executive chair behind it. There was a pair of matching leather chairs to this side of the desk with a sturdy round table in between. The place was dark and looked like a room in a 1950s men's club. It seemed out of place with the rest of the house but said a whole lot about Duncan Hayes's good old boy's personality.

"Come around to this side," Marla said, walking

around the big desk and then perching on the edge of the executive chair. She tapped on the keyboard, and the monitor sitting on the desk sprung to life. She pointed to the document that filled the screen. "See this? It's a contract that says Duncan Hayes is a silent partner in Bynum Ross's business. This name has been blocked out, but there's a third person involved."

"Can I drive for a second?" Emerson asked. She was decent with computers and thought she might be able to remove the block on the name.

"Sure." Marla hopped up and stepped aside almost immediately.

After a few keystrokes, Emerson unblocked the name. "Mortimer Turner."

Emerson immediately looked at Marla, whose eyes were huge. "Turner. That might be the M Turn you're looking for." And then the name of the bait and tackle shop smacked her in the forehead. "B-T. I thought it stood for Bait and Tackle. What if it's a play on initials? What if it stands for Bynum and Turner?"

After she was quickly briefed on the event that had made them late, Marla shook her head. She gasped.

"That's it," she said. "I'm calling Bynum."

The first thing Emerson wanted to do was give Rory an update. She glanced around like he was standing there but remembered he was still outside with Leah, and rightfully so. Emerson had grown accustomed to having him by her side, so his absence was a huge void in her world.

Marla made the call, and then put them on speaker.

"Bynum Ross," she started with the voice of a second-grade teacher about to give a serious scolding. "What have you done?"

"Ma'am," Bynum said with respect and a little bit of fear that had been missing from his voice when he spoke to Emerson.

"I've seen the legal documents with you, my father-in-law and Morty Turner," she said. "I'm about to call in the sheriff but thought I'd give you a chance to explain yourself first."

There was a long, intense silence on the phone.

"Will you let me explain before you do?" Bynum asked.

"Yes," Marla huffed.

"I'm on my way," Bynum said.

"I'VE REGRETTED MY ACTIONS, RORY," Leah said as she planted a hand on the wall to steady herself as he flipped through the photos on his cell phone. "She's got your eyes and mouth."

"It's a good thing she didn't get my nose," he said as the tension started to dissipate.

"She's beautiful," Leah said with so much admiration and respect in her voice he couldn't help but let go of some of the anger he'd been harboring.

"And she's smart," he pointed out. "Not exactly straight As but she tries subjects she isn't sure she'll be good at just for the challenge, which I think is a good thing."

Leah nodded and smiled. It was interesting to note how people's past decisions had a way of defining them, aging them, changing them. Regret was heavy; he of all people would know. The weight could drag a person below the surface, have them fighting for air to keep from drowning.

"I'm a terrible person for walking out on you the way I did, let alone our daughter." Tears sprang to her eyes again. The concern lines deepened, and it was evident that she'd been beating herself up for a long time over this, paddling, trying to keep her head above water. He didn't have it in him to push her under. Too many times people took the shot when they should be offering a hand up instead.

Setting his own hurt aside, he said, "We were kids. What did we know?"

"You didn't run away," she said. "And now you've brought up an amazing human whereas I've missed it all."

"Only up to this point," he said. "Plus, I have a ridiculous amount of pictures and videos. Maybe you and Liv can watch them together someday. I'm sure she'd get a kick out of it."

"Do you think she wants to see me?" Leah asked, a mix of hope and trepidation in her eyes.

"I haven't asked her yet, but I'd bet money on it," he reassured. "I could have done a better job of staying in touch instead of licking my wounds all these years, Leah."

"It wasn't your responsibility," she said.

"We cared about each other a great deal at one time," he pointed out. "So much so that we got married and tried to do 'the right thing' by Liv. Point being, you cared enough to try even though it scared us both like crazy."

"You didn't abandon her," she said. "I did that. And you. I left you, Rory, and I still can't find a good reason as to why." She put a hand up. "I'm not hung up on us now. We've both moved on. But I guess you never stop caring about your first love."

"You're the mother of my child, Leah. That will always mean something special to me," he said to her.

"Hearing that means the world, Rory," she said. "And if Liv would like to meet me someday, I would love that."

"I'll talk to her before we firm up plans, but we haven't had a trip to Austin in a while. She'll have a week off from school for Thanksgiving. Since the holiday is coming up maybe we can swing down and grab a cup of coffee with you and your family." Knowing Liv like he did, she would jump at the chance to visit an Austin coffee shop. Plus, coming from San Antonio would be a short drive for Leah allowing them to meet on equal ground. Liv might even buy another Longhorn sweater while in town since UT was her dream school. At least for now. She was only twelve and had a few more years before making college decisions and he was in no hurry for her to grow up. He'd take as much time as he could get with his little girl.

"That would be amazing," Leah said with the brightest smile. She looked lighter somehow, or maybe the years came off in conjunction with her relief. "If she wants to."

"I'm going to step out on faith here and say she will," he said.

Leah glanced around and then patted her pockets like she was looking for something and then suddenly realized it wasn't on her. "I've been writing letters to her every year. Christmas, birthdays, etc. They're in my car." She seemed to search his gaze. "Do you think she would want them?"

"I do," he said, walking her over to her car.

She pulled out a flowery hat-sized box. "I've written every year on big occasions in case she ever wanted to know me when I'm gone." A tear spilled down her cheeks. "I just never imagined this would happen now. I thought maybe when I'm..." She waved her hand a couple of times like they were magic wands that could somehow wipe away the tears. "All I can say is thank you."

"Everyone deserves a second chance, Leah." He meant those words too. As long as the person had changed and was committed to doing better, he didn't have it in his heart to shut them down.

"I'd hug you but I don't want to make your wife jealous," Leah said. He must have shot her a look because her gaze dropped to his ring finger. "Or whatever the two of you are."

The word *friend* didn't seem right to describe his

relationship with Emerson, so he didn't say anything. Instead, he handed over his cell phone and asked her to enter her contact information.

"Could I have a picture of her to show my husband and son?" Leah asked.

He nodded.

"I better get back and relieve the babysitter," Leah said. She gave him an earnest look. "I honestly don't know how you did all this by yourself, especially starting out so young."

"You figure it out," he said. "Plus, I got lucky with the greatest kid."

Leah smiled. She looked hopeful and more at peace since he first saw her a little while ago, and it was a good look on her.

Rory stood in the parking lot as she slipped into her vehicle and drove away after handing his cell phone back. His thoughts shifted to Emerson and her mother. He'd seen the fear in Emerson's eye that her mother wouldn't want anything to do with her even though Emerson was moving heaven and earth to find the woman. The meeting would have to be one of the scariest moments in a person's life. The possibility of rejection from a person who was supposed to offer unconditional love would be hard to face. He was gutted at the possibility Emerson's mother might not want to meet her. Either way, Emerson had gained a new family now. They would stand with her as much as she needed them to.

His heart went out to the person who had helped

him see, so clearly, that Liv needed to have the option to have a relationship with her mother. After seeing Leah, he realized it was the right thing to do for her too. The time had come to move past the hurt inflicted by teenagers on each other. They were all adults now, capable of healing the past. He owed a great debt to Emerson for helping him see it.

And now, more than anything, he wanted to be the one to help her find her mother. He hoped for the best but at the very least, she might get closure.

As Leah's car disappeared down the road, he fished out his cell phone and called Liv. She was out of school by now and had already sent three texts.

"Hey, Dad," she practically chirped. "What's up?" Liv calling him Dad instead of Daddy was a new thing. He wasn't sure he liked it since it meant she was shedding all things that made him feel like she was still his little girl.

"I have a serious question for you," he said. "And you can be honest with me."

"Oh, seriously? Okay," she said and he could envision her sitting up a little straighter. "What is it?"

"Do you ever think about your mom? Or have questions? Because you used to ask about her when you were little and you stopped, and I kind of left the subject alone," he said.

She paused, almost like she was trying to find the right words. Was she worried she might hurt his feelings if she wanted to know about her mother?

"I mean, sure," she said. "But it doesn't mean anything."

"It's okay," he reassured her. "I would be worried if you didn't think about her sometimes."

"Well, my friends do ask about her and I kind of don't really know what to say to them, but it's no big deal or anything," she said, stumbling a bit on her words. He knew she was trying to protect him. She did care and it was a big deal; she just didn't feel comfortable admitting it.

"How would you like to get to know her?" he asked.

"What? How? Is that, like, even possible?" Liv asked.

"Yes, it is. We've gotten in touch here recently and I thought it might be nice if the two of you met. Got to know each other a little bit."

"You wouldn't mind? Because, like, I have so many questions."

"I can put the two of you in touch right now or you can wait until the break and we can meet her in Austin for coffee," he said.

"And you would be there? In Austin?" she asked. "You would come with me?"

"Right by your side," he said, a knot forming in his throat, making it difficult to swallow. "Always."

"That would be amazing," she squealed.

"I'll set it up," he said as another vehicle came up the drive. "I have to go, but I'll be home as soon as I can."

"Love you, Daddy," Liv said. For a moment, she was his little girl again.

"Love you too," he said before adding, "Now, go do your homework."

"When have I not?" He could almost hear the eye roll come through the line.

Rory chuckled, feeling a lightness he hadn't felt in far too long. The feeling faded when he got a good look at the driver of the approaching vehicle.

What was Bynum Ross doing here?

Chapter Twenty

Emerson resisted the urge to run outside and give Bynum Ross a piece of her mind. Instead, she stayed in the kitchen with Granny while Marla went to greet the man, the click of her shoes reverberating on the tile floor.

From the window, she could see Rory standing in the parking lot with a flowery hat box tucked underneath his arm, right fist on his hip. His chest was out like he was bucked up for a fight and she could almost feel the tension radiating off him from here.

The front door opened and then closed, but she could hear a pin drop in the house otherwise. Granny picked that moment to tap her fingers on the table and at least it provided some background noise for distraction.

"Coffee?" Emerson asked Granny.

"Might as well," she said. "Worst case, we can throw the cups at Bynum's head if he gets sassy."

"He wasn't nice to me when I stopped by the bait and tackle shop," Emerson said as she moved around the granite island. "And then I'm about ninety-nine percent certain he sent someone to run me off of the road, or worse. The truck caused me to crash my Bronco and that's where Rory stepped in."

Granny's finger tapping picked up speed.

Emerson poured two coffee mugs and brought them back to the table. "I forgot to ask if you like anything in your coffee."

"Black is fine," Granny said. Her finger tapping moved to the side of the mug. Her lips compressed, forming a thin line, and her gaze narrowed. "Bynum had better watch himself is all I can say."

From the window, Emerson saw him park and then walk toward Rory and Marla. Rory's mother immediately turned toward the house and the three proceeded to the back door with Bynum bringing up the rear. Rory broke off long enough to put the box inside his truck and then jogged up in time to walk in right behind Bynum. All signs of anger were gone from his face as he entered the kitchen. Marla was one of the most polite hostesses on the planet from what Emerson had seen so far, so it was telling when she didn't so much as ask the man to sit.

"You had better start explaining," Marla said, whirling around on Bynum as he reached the edge of the granite island. He backed up a step and then his hands came up in the surrender position.

"I wasn't trying to do anything wrong, and the other day wasn't personal." He gestured toward Emerson, which made her blood boil.

"Oh, really?" Emerson said through gritted teeth. "How is being a complete jerk to me and then sending someone to—what…take care of me, kill me— not being personal? Because it feels very personal."

"Hold on there a minute," Bynum defended, puffing out his chest and pulling up his pants using both hands to readjust at the waistline. "I most definitely wasn't trying to kill anybody." He exhaled and put the palm of his hand on the granite island like it was an anchor keeping him from floating out to sea. "All I was trying to do was scare you a little bit. Get you to get out of town and give up on your search. You weren't supposed to be seriously hurt."

"My aunt is in the hospital right now. If Rory and I hadn't arrived when we did today, she would be dead," Emerson bit out. It was difficult to reconcile the Bynum standing here with the one who'd been so intent on being a bastard to her in his store.

The look of shock on Bynum's face convinced her that he had no idea what she was talking about. Was he a good actor? Did he send someone who went off the rails?

"You sent someone to strangle her. Why?" Emerson continued. "What did she do?"

"Hold on," Bynum started backing up until the counter stopped him. He was shaking his head. His eyes were wide. "I don't have the first idea what you're talking about."

Rory's fists were clenched at his sides. Marla held up her cell phone. But it was Granny who stood up, crossed the room and poked her index finger into Bynum's chest.

"I've known you and your family for a very long time, Bynum," she said. "You look me in the eyes and tell me the truth or my daughter will let the sheriff sort out this mess."

Bynum raised his right hand as though he was about to take an oath. "I promise that I have no idea what happened to this young lady's aunt. I was awful to her when she came into my shop the other day to protect someone who I happen to care a whole lot about. I gave my word that I would do whatever it took to protect this person's whereabouts. If Duncan was here right now, he would back me up because it's the reason he went into business with me. He bought out my partner on paper."

"Where are the profits?" Marla said. "I haven't seen any deposits in any of Duncan's accounts from B-T. How is it possible he's a partner if there's no money?"

"There is money," Bynum said. "Duncan was a partner in name only. I split the profits and deposit into a separate account. One you wouldn't know about because it goes to someone we promised to protect after Morty Turner died."

"Sounds fishy if you ask me," Granny said, taking a few steps back and crossing her arms over her chest.

"I can prove it," Bynum said. "My accountant can verify everything I'm saying is true."

"If Morty Turner is dead, who gets his half of the money?" Rory asked. "Did he have a wife?"

Bynum stood there for a long moment with his lips pursed like he was on the verge of spilling a name and had to clamp his mouth closed to stop himself. And then he turned his attention to Emerson. He stared for a long moment and then shook his head.

"You look so much like her," he finally said. "I knew the second you walked into my shop who you belonged to. She was pretty and had those same eyes. The same long blond hair like that young actress Amanda something from the movie…"

"Seyfried," Marla supplied.

"That's the one," he said. "You got those from your mother."

"You know her?" Emerson couldn't contain her shock.

"I did," he admitted.

"And now?" she asked, worried that her mother was already gone before the two had a chance to meet.

"Couldn't tell you where she is or what she does, but those deposits are automatic," he said. "I can give you the account information and you can follow up from there." He turned to Marla with pleading eyes. "I'd appreciate keeping all of this out of the sheriff's office. An investigation would bring a whole lot of light onto my financial dealings and I'd like to keep this arrangement out of the news, far away from public record."

Marla nodded.

"I can't promise not to bring the sheriff in at all," Marla said. "But I do acknowledge what you're saying and I won't make the call unless I have to."

"Wait. Why did any of this need to be arranged in the first place?" Emerson asked, thinking her mother must have ended up in witness protection or something.

Bynum cursed.

"It was because of your father," he said through clenched teeth. "He's responsible for all of this. He caused Naomi to go into hiding."

The revelation was like a bomb detonating inside Emerson's brain. The air in the room thinned and something as simple as taking in air was next to impossible. Her lungs clawed for air. She needed to breathe.

Emerson made a run for the back door as tears streamed down her cheeks. Her father wasn't the overprotective man she remembered…because if this was true, he was a monster.

Rory went after Emerson. There was no way he was letting her deal with this alone if she would allow him to be there for her. She pushed through the back door and took off running. He followed, leaving her plenty of room in case she needed it.

By the time she stopped, his lungs burned and his thighs screamed. He stayed far enough back to give her space.

"I should probably be in there right now peppering

Bynum with questions about what he knows about my mother and how he knows my father is responsible," she finally said while still gasping for air. "But I couldn't."

He didn't respond. He just listened to her as he tried to steady his own pulse. As it was, his heart pounded the inside of his ribs.

"This is the man who raised me," she continued. "I always looked up to him in so many ways even though looking back his overprotectiveness was probably for the wrong reasons. As annoying as it had been, I just interpreted it as a father's love. How wrong was I?"

"As a parent, I can tell you there's no rule book," Rory stated. "That being said, I think his actions showed that he loved you, even if he was awful to your mother or made her life unbearable."

"He pushed her away and into hiding, Rory. What kind of a person does that?" she asked, bending over and placing her hands on her knees as she took in a few deep breaths.

"I can't and won't defend his actions," Rory admitted. "I'm not even sure what we're dealing with here and, I'll admit, it doesn't sound good. But he wouldn't have kept you if he didn't love you. That's not a question in my mind."

She tilted her head toward him and he could see that she was listening.

"And your mother might have been forced away from you, meaning it wasn't her choice," he pointed

out. "Which also means she wanted to be with you."
He was going out on a limb but still believed those
words to be true. A picture was emerging. And, besides, who wouldn't love Emerson? Liv was always
guarded with new people and she'd already texted
to say how much she liked Emerson. There were a
whole bunch of heart emojis involved in the conversation, which he saw as a good thing.

Plus, if he had another daughter who was like Emerson, he couldn't imagine not loving her.

"Do you believe that Bynum isn't responsible for
what happened to my aunt?" she asked.

"I knew him growing up here and didn't know
him to be a liar," he said. "Then, there's Duncan to
consider. He might have been hard-core in a whole
lot of ways but he prized honesty. And he would go
to the ends of the earth to protect someone he cared
about. It sounds like my grandfather was in business with Bynum before he died. The arrangement
makes sense based on the people who are involved.
I'm not defending any of it, though. And I certainly
wouldn't want to condone anything that hurt you. It
sounds like your father had all the power and your
mother had no choice but to disappear. Those men
wouldn't protect just anyone. They had to care about
her to put themselves on the line the way they did."

Her tense expression eased and he could see the
wheels turning.

"Still, would you be able to walk away from Liv?"
she asked. "I mean, under the same circumstances.

Would you just turn your back on your daughter like that?"

"That's not a fair question," he said. "My life has never depended on walking away from my daughter. It would be too easy for me to sit back and judge another person's decisions or mistakes, but that wouldn't be fair."

"You're probably right," she said but he could hear the pain in her voice.

"Let's find your mother and hear her out," he said. "But first, let's figure out who went after your aunt."

Someone out there wanted to keep the secret buried. They were willing to kill in order to protect the past.

Emerson chewed on her bottom lip, a sure sign she was contemplating his idea. It didn't take too long for her to nod. "Let's head back while Bynum is still here. I have questions and he seems to be in a talkative mood."

"I'm just wondering who went after your aunt, if not him," Rory stated. The thought didn't exactly evoke a whole lot of warm and fuzzy feelings. She was still in real danger if Bynum wasn't responsible for the attack. The man seemed just as shocked by the event as they'd been. The Arlington police were on the job, searching for the runner. Her aunt was safe in the hospital, being watched over.

Could Bynum lead them to Emerson's mother? It seemed she held the answers—answers that still must be relevant after all this time because she'd been in hiding nearly thirty years. What could have been so horrible that she would need to go underground all this time? Did she know her former husband was gone? And if she did, why hadn't she resurfaced?

Emerson's father recently passed away. It was possible her mother hadn't received the news. Considering Bynum didn't seem to have an address for her or any way to contact her directly, she might be so deep in hiding no one would be able to find her. Rory's heart ached at the thought Emerson might never get the answers she needed to move on. Talking to Leah and being able to clear the air brought healing to a wound that had felt open and raw.

The notion Emerson might never get that broke his heart.

"We have a name and bank account information," he said to Emerson as they turned toward the main house and started to trek back. "It's something to go on."

"What if she doesn't want to be found?" she said. "She could be so deep in hiding that I might never find her."

"We'll search for her like it's our job," he reassured. "We can hire folks who know how."

"I can't help but wonder what my father did to cause her to run away like that," she said.

"Let's find out," he said. "If I've learned anything lately, it's that things aren't always as they seem and it's damaging to draw conclusions about anyone without all the facts. I've also learned that people make mistakes that haunt them the rest of their lives if they don't find a way to clear the air and move past them."

Emerson nodded but didn't speak. She was chewing on her bottom lip again, which meant the wheels were turning. The problem was that she was holding it all inside and not talking to him. His old insecurities reared their heads and he dreaded the moment when she would walk out on him too.

Chapter Twenty-One

"How can I find her or get a message to her?" Emerson asked Bynum, who was now seated at the kitchen table nursing a cup of fresh brew and looking sorrowful and defeated.

"Your guess is as good as mine," he said. "We tried to call the bank since I make the deposits to get information and they refused."

"That's not all that surprising," she said. "Can they pass along an email? Or forward a handwritten note?"

"I can ask," he said, then picked up his cell phone. He made the call while they were all in the room. He said "thank you" a few times after making his case, then said, "I understand. Yes, an email would work fine." Then came a pause. "Right. No promises."

He ended the call and looked at Emerson. "They'll accept an email but can't confirm whether any withdrawals have been made from the account."

"It's better than nothing," she said as his cell dinged.

"They just texted the bank manager's email address." He held out his cell so that Emerson could retrieve hers and transfer the information.

"Hold on a second," she said, moving to the island. She set her phone on top and then crafted a message to her mother, giving a quick rundown of recent events and what had happened with Aunt Ginny. She closed by saying she might be in danger and needed her mother's help. She asked her to meet across the street from the B&B tomorrow night at dusk if she can or suggest another time, date and location. Before she hit Send, she added the words, "Would really like to meet you."

Hitting Send on the email was one of the most unnerving things she'd ever done. Her heart raced, her pulse skyrocketed and fear flooded her. It was now or never, so she took a deep breath, mentally put on her big-girl panties and tapped the screen.

"Why did my mother have to go into hiding?" she asked Bynum straight out.

He stared at the rim of his coffee cup.

"You must know the reason if you were willing to go to this degree to protect her," she said.

"It's just stirring up a hornet's nest to keep going down this track," he stated with an apologetic look. Apology or not, she needed him to talk.

"I think that ship has sailed," she said to him. "My aunt could have died this morning if we hadn't decided to take a detour and stop by to ask a few questions before heading back down here." Now that she really thought about it, she could go to her aunt's house and go through her things to see if she could find the truth. "My vehicle is in the shop right now. It was broken into."

"They're looking for proof," he said. "They must believe you know something."

"Who is *they*?" she asked. He brought his gaze up to meet hers and she held steady. "You already admitted my father is involved." It dawned on her the man had lived a double life.

"Bad idea," Bynum said. "I wish you could leave it all alone for your own safety."

"Again, it's too late for that," she said,

"Look what they did to your mother," he fired back before putting his face in his hands. "Do you think they won't do the same thing to you? If you leave it alone now, there might be hope. I can spread word that you don't know anything so there'll be no reason to come after you."

"If you're trying to scare me off, it won't work," she said, steady in her determination to uncover the truth.

"Are you really willing to risk everything?" His gaze shifted from her to Rory and back so fast she almost missed it. "To leave your life behind on a moment's notice? Because your father didn't act alone, and his partner won't rest until there's no way to tie the crimes back to either one of them. Lives are on the line and yours will be inconsequential to these folks. You can't possibly want to bring that into your life."

"What if we go after the bastard instead?" Rory

cut in. "Make sure the son of a bitch spends the rest of his days behind bars?"

"That's a tall order," Bynum said. "Are you willing to risk her life?"

"No," Rory immediately snapped. "But what is the alternative?"

"Go to the sheriff, for one," Marla interrupted, waving her hands in the air.

"How is he doing with the threat to the ranch?" Bynum asked pointedly.

Marla's cheeks turned fire-engine red. "Rory hasn't been brought up to speed on the issue yet."

"Is that why you've been calling us all home?" Rory asked before saying, "Never mind. Let's stay on topic for right now. But that subject isn't closed."

"It's under control," Marla said.

"For now," Granny, who had so far been quiet, said.

Emerson made a loop around the granite island. She tucked a loose tendril of hair behind her ear.

"The way I see it, I'm already in the hot seat," she began, thinking out loud. "Otherwise, this wouldn't have happened to my aunt. Plus, someone was lurking around my home last night. I'm wondering now if it was the same person from this morning with Aunt Ginny."

"I suppose it's possible." Bynum shrugged his shoulders. "The cat might already be out of the bag on this one, in which case you need to watch your back."

"Did my mother ever tell you what she found

out?" Emerson asked. There must be evidence or it would have been her word against theirs.

Bynum shook his head. "All she said was that it was bad and no one needed to ask questions but she needed to disappear."

"Did she say anything about me?" Emerson regretted the question as soon as it left her mouth. Bynum would have said something by now if her mother had been heartsick about leaving her infant daughter.

"All she said was the man she married wasn't who she thought he was and she was forced to give up everything to escape him. This person was cruel and not at all like the one who swooped into town and stole her heart," he explained. "Your mother couldn't wait to get off the ranch and 'experience life' as she'd put it all those years ago. Back then, the business barely made enough for us to make ends meet. Their family's ranch was a couple of towns over and had fallen on hard times after three years of drought and no water rights. Bit by bit, they sold off their livestock and then put a mortgage on the place to start B-T. Times were lean in the early years, but we made do and now we do okay. She's comfortable."

Emerson's own flesh and blood could turn her back on her. After thinking about Liv and the connection she had with Rory, tears threatened. Even Leah regretted walking away from Liv, which probably gave Emerson hope her mother did the same. If it was true, she would have mentioned Emerson.

Maybe it was time to face the reality her mother didn't care. A child was made up of parts from two other human beings. Did Emerson remind her mother too much of her father to ever truly love her?

Bynum's cell dinged, interrupting the heavy conversation. He checked the screen. "The bank has confirmed the email was delivered."

Which was no guarantee she would show tomorrow.

"I'VE SAID MY PIECE," Bynum said, pushing off the table to standing. "I apologize for any harm I've caused. No one from my camp will try to run you off the road again."

"Or break into her vehicle," Rory growled.

"I don't know what you're talking about there," Bynum said. "That wasn't my doing."

He walked over to where Emerson stood behind the granite island and lowered his voice so low Rory almost couldn't hear. "Your mother was…is…a good person who got mixed up with the wrong person. I haven't seen or heard from her in decades, but that doesn't mean I don't care or wonder how she's doing from time to time. Either way, I make the deposits and will continue to do so until otherwise notified." He turned to Rory. "Your grandfather was a good man. I miss him every day."

With that, Bynum leaned in as though going for a hug. The surprise move seemed to catch Emerson off guard. Her body stiffened at first, and then she appeared to relax into the embrace.

"She would have wanted me to do that," Bynum said after pulling back. "And, if I may say so, I believe she would be proud of the young woman you've become."

"Thank you for saying." Emerson's eyes watered, and her chin quivered. She turned around to face the window behind the sink when Bynum left the room.

Granny quietly stood up and walked over to Emerson, gently patting her on the back like only a grandmother could do, the gesture offering comfort.

The request to meet her mother had been sent. Delivery had been confirmed. Beyond that, there wasn't much else that could be done other than check on her aunt. Rory thought about the former special ops folks who started security and protection or runaway/abduction locator businesses. He had enough money saved to hire any one of them. Would a trail somehow lead back to Naomi? Would he bring death to her doorstep?

The risk wasn't worth it, not since contact had been made. Now, the ball was in her mother's court.

Patience wasn't exactly Rory's most prized trait. He convinced himself a long time ago that was the reason he'd been a success at a young age. He didn't sit around and wait for something to happen. He *made* things happen with action. It went against his nature to stand back and let a situation unfold. But that was exactly what he had to do in this case no matter how tense it made him.

The rest of the evening was quiet. Emerson slipped outside after dinner dishes had been put away, without drawing attention to herself. Rory ended up alone with his mother in the kitchen for the first time since he'd been home.

"I thought Callum and Payton were staying here," he said to his mom as she finished wiping down the counter. She could have hired help a long time ago but preferred to do everything for herself. She said no one would care about her home the way she did. There was probably some truth to her statement.

"They're in Houston this week and next," his mom said, glancing at the wall calendar. "He's the happiest I've ever seen him."

Rory wasn't sure if that was meant to be a hint about his situation with Emerson. Rather than address the comment, he moved on. "Tell me what's going on at the ranch."

"Someone has been threatening us since your grandfather passed away," she admitted. "Since Callum is splitting his time here, it's been quiet. We're keeping an eye on the situation, but right now it's calm."

"I wish you'd said something before," he stated, even though he understood why she'd kept it to herself.

"Right now, you have enough on your plate," she

said. "And, besides, I can't wait to meet my granddaughter."

"She's going to love you as much as I do," he said.

"I hope so. The girls in this family have always been outnumbered. It's time to even the score with the next generation." She winked and laughed. It was good to see her smiling.

"Where do you want us tonight?" he asked.

"Callum and Payton have taken over the guest suite downstairs," his mom said. "Why don't you guys take your old room in the west wing?"

"I haven't been in that old room since high school," he said.

"Not much has changed," she said. "You never were one for putting posters on the wall or fussing over decorations. Furniture is the same since we redecorated at the beginning of high school."

"Since *you* redecorated. I was good with the old stuff," he teased.

"You gave me a hard time about that, but I did it for everyone the summer before high school. Figured you might feel like sticking around if I got rid of the Batman sheets," she quipped.

"Now, I see the grand scheme," he said with a chuckle. "And it was Spider-Man."

The memory brought a spark to her eyes that had been missing when he first walked through the door. She morphed into serious mode when she nodded toward the window. "It's okay if you want to go check on her."

"Was I that obvious?" he asked.

"You've glanced at the window six times in the last minute. Go on."

"I love you, Mom," he said, kissing her on top of the head.

"I love you too, Rory."

Hearing those words in person instead of on the phone or through a text overwhelmed him with good feelings. Being home was good and he wanted to do more of this. He was starting to see the vision of big family holidays, cookies baking, family all around. Liv would be here with the biggest smile on her face as she learned how to bake Granny's gingerbread cookies. Emerson was here, mug in hand, sampling treats and...

He stopped himself before he went too far down that road. Emerson was special and he needed a minute to figure out what that meant. It also dawned on Rory that he'd let Duncan Hayes take the good of this place away from him and Liv, and he vowed never to let that happen again.

As he moved to the back door, it opened. Emerson walked inside. One look at her verified she needed rest. Without a word spoken between them, he took her by the hand and walked her upstairs to the room they would be sharing tonight. He could take the oversize chair next to the windows in one corner of the room.

"Bathroom is attached." He pointed to the door. "This place is always ready for company, so there should be supplies in there. I'll run down and grab your bag from the truck."

By the time he returned, the shower was already going. He opened the door enough to slide her bag inside, figuring she needed pajamas and the rest of her stuff. He had no idea what went on inside those walls, but Liv kept a whole lot of products on the counter.

He looked around his old room. There were still clothes hanging in the walk-in closet from more than a decade ago. He bet they still fit. There were T-shirts, button-downs and jeans. He had several pairs of boots, sports shoes and plain running shoes. Being inside his old room didn't bring back a whole lot of memories, but his closet sure did. All those years of sports came rushing back. More good memories too. He must have locked it all away for his own sanity.

The door to the bathroom opened and he could hear Emerson step into the bedroom. He walked over to the bed and turned down the comforter.

"Make yourself comfortable," he said to her as she set her bag on a chair next to the dresser. "I should only be a minute."

She nodded and offered a forced smile.

Rory took a quick shower and threw on a pair of light cotton drawstring pajama pants. He cut off the light, surprised to find all the lights still on in the next room. Emerson sat up in bed with the covers across her lap and pillows fluffed behind her.

"Hold me tonight?" she asked. The effect those three words had on him told him how much trouble he was in as he climbed in beside her and pulled her against his chest as they lay down.

Rory was in deep, and he wouldn't apologize for it.

Chapter Twenty-Two

Emerson didn't wake up until noon the next day. The first thing she did after freshening up in the bathroom was to call the hospital and check on her aunt. Ginny was doing fine and was expected to make a full recovery. She was sleeping when Emerson called, so she made a mental note to call back later.

Hunger forced her to throw on a sports bra underneath her T-shirt and then head downstairs. The home was so big, she got turned around and somehow ended up back at Duncan Hayes's office.

She turned and headed back in the opposite direction toward the kitchen. Rory's deep timbre encouraged her to pick up the pace.

He was in the kitchen alone walking around with his phone like he was giving a virtual tour. She figured Liv was the lucky recipient. She slipped quietly into the room.

He must have heard her because he immediately turned to her and smiled.

"Emerson's here," he said and turned the screen to

face her. Emerson closed the distance between them. The sweet face on the phone momentarily brightened her mood.

"Hi," she said to Liv, whose face lit up.

"Emerson," Liv said, the excitement in the girl's voice making her feel like she'd just hit the lotto. How could anyone be in a bad mood around that kid?

"Why aren't you in school?" Emerson asked, realizing she just sounded like a parent and wondering where that came from. She hadn't envisioned kids for herself but she would be honored to have someone like Liv for a daughter.

"Half day," Liv said, her smile brightening. "Some of us woke up before noon today."

Emerson laughed despite herself.

"You got me there," she said. "Which is why I need to head to the coffee machine."

"Don't go," Liv whined. "Not before you help me pick out an outfit."

"Okay," Emerson said. "What are the choices?"

"Hold on." Liv's cell phone fell back and suddenly they were looking at the chandelier in what Emerson assumed was the kid's bedroom. She returned, propped up the phone and then held a hanger with a flowery minidress up against her body.

"Oh, that's cute," Emerson said as Rory shook his head off camera. She couldn't help but smile.

"You think?" Liv said. "I could wear it with these." She picked up a pair of shiny black combat boots. "Or these." The second choice was high-top tennis shoes.

"I like the combat boots," Emerson said. "Definitely the combat boots."

"Where do you plan to wear this outfit to?" Rory cut in.

"Coffee shop," Liv said with enthusiasm.

"Aren't you too young for caffeine?" Rory asked in a disapproving father tone.

"I'm almost thirteen," Liv defended. "You said I could start drinking coffee when I was a teenager."

"That's when you were five years old and weren't supposed to remember." He knew he was busted.

Liv rolled her eyes. "I have another outfit."

"Okay," Emerson said. "Let's see it."

"Keep an open mind, all right?" Liv disappeared before either of them could say a word. She came back on-screen with a shiny neon orange number that would leave more skin exposed than the back of a hospital gown.

"That's a hard no," Rory said, handing over the phone and heading toward the coffee machine.

"Dad," Liv whined.

"I like the first one the best because I think it makes you look older," Emerson reasoned.

"You do?" Liv asked.

"You look more mature," Emerson said. "It has more street style."

"Yeah, I guess that's true," Liv said, seriously contemplating Emerson's opinion.

"The colors are better for your skin tone too,"

Emerson continued. "The other one will wash you out too much."

"Oh, right," Liv said. "Outfit number one it is."

Rory turned around and mouthed a thank-you.

"I'm going to give you back to your dad," Emerson said.

"Got it," Liv said before adding, "It's nice to have a woman's point of view. Thank you."

Those words weren't off-the-charts sentimental but they sure made Emerson choke up. "It's good talking to you."

Coffee, lunch and a walk around the property pretty much made up the day. Emerson wasn't in a talkative mood and she appreciated Rory being nearby but giving her space at the same time.

"If you want to get there early, we should head out now," Rory said around four. This time of year, it got dark around five thirty and they would need time to get into town.

"I'll change and be right down," Emerson said. She found their room again and then changed into jeans and a light sweater. She had no idea if there was a proper outfit for meeting her mother but also realized she might be stood up, so she figured no need going through too much trouble. She slicked her hair back in a low ponytail and threw on a little lip gloss and concealer.

She glanced at the bed on the way downstairs. Last night had been the best sleep she'd had in longer than she could remember. Rory Hayes was dangerous to her heart because he felt a little too much like home.

At four on the dot, they were inside his truck. Another forty minutes, they were in town. The day had been quiet. Almost too quiet. Her nerves were strung tight.

"She'll show," Rory finally said as he pulled into the B&B's parking lot.

"How do you know?" Emerson asked. "She could have emailed me back. I've been thinking about the fact she didn't and I'm okay if my mother wants nothing to do with me. At the very least, I've been in contact. She knows I'm interested in seeing her. The ball's in her court. I tried and after this, if she doesn't show, I can walk away knowing I did what I could to reach out to her."

"Don't give up hope if today doesn't work out," he said. "There could be other reasons at play, like she could get held up in traffic."

"Wouldn't she email to let me know if that was the case?" she asked, thinking he was truly a good person for wanting to shield her from the potential pain coming her way.

"Unless we can ask her outright, we don't know anything for certain," he said. "I'd just hate for you to prematurely close a door. That's all."

"I appreciate you saying so, but not everyone gets their happy ending like you and Liv. Some people live in the real world where parents reject their own children," Emerson said with more than a little frustration in her tone. She wished she could reel those words back in as soon as they left her mouth. "I'm sorry. I shouldn't take my irritation out on you."

"You didn't mean any harm," he said even though she heard a twinge of hurt in his voice. "Don't apologize."

A moment of silence sat heavy between them. She wanted to clear the air but didn't know how.

He exited the vehicle and went around the front to open her door. She saw him survey the area across the street. There were two cars parked at the B&B, more at the café next door.

Emerson immediately studied the area the minute she was outside the vehicle. There was no movement across the street. Her pulse kicked up a few notches with every step away from the truck and toward the meetup area.

Rory reached for her hand, linking their fingers. She calmed to a level below panic. Strange how much she cared about the opinion of someone she didn't even know. When she thought about it like that, it didn't make sense to be nervous.

A deputy's vehicle went flying past. Rory tightened his grip on her fingers before taking off toward the truck.

"What's happening?" Emerson asked.

"Let's find out."

RORY COULDN'T GET behind the wheel fast enough. His seat belt barely clicked before he fired up the engine and was backing out of the parking spot. The deputy most likely was headed toward Jimmy's place.

There was no way Rory would catch up, but that wouldn't stop him from trying.

"Stay close to me once I park, okay?" he asked Emerson.

"Okay," she said as they barreled down the street.

Jimmy's place wasn't far. There were a couple of unmarked vehicles with lights swirling parked out front. Rory slowed down and parked a block away, figuring they could get a good look around the back of the building and get the drop on what was going on.

This time, Emerson reached for his hand after exiting the vehicle. He led her down the back of the small strip center. Jimmy's garage was on the end. As they rounded the corner to the side of the building, Emerson tugged at his hand.

"The truck," she whispered.

Sure enough, there was a truck parked behind the garbage bins. They moved toward it, figuring there wasn't much time to investigate if the Feds were already inside the building.

A groan sounded as they passed by the bins. Emerson tugged Rory back a step. He tucked her behind him and then opened the bin to find Theo Harlingen inside. His face was swollen and his nose was bleeding.

"Theo?" Rory said to the unmoving deputy. "Wake up, buddy."

Theo blinked and squinted despite there being very little light left. His mouth opened and he seemed to struggle to say the word. Then came, "Jimmy."

A hard, blunt object slammed into the back of Emerson's head. Her eyes closed and her body went limp.

Chapter Twenty-Three

Rory twisted around in time to grab Emerson before she hit the concrete. In saving her, he took a blunt force blow to the side of his head. He ducked enough to miss some of the impact, then had to gently set Emerson down on her side.

When he came up, he brought fury with him.

"Jimmy, you son of a—"

Rory dived at Jimmy's legs. The tire iron in his hand flew out as a snap sounded in his kneecaps. Rory had a solid thirty pounds of muscle on a skinnier Jimmy, who hit the pavement hard. He was wiry and determined.

Wriggling and writhing on the cracked cement, Jimmy almost wiggled out of Rory's grip.

"What are you doing? What do you have to do with any of this?" Rory asked through grunts as he fought to get Jimmy's arms under control again.

"Why do you care?" Jimmy asked. "You abandoned your family and never looked back. You should stay in the city where you belong."

"What is that supposed to mean?" Rory asked,

and then it dawned on him. "Your dad was the other person involved, wasn't he?"

"Family is everything," Jimmy repeated, landing a knee in Rory's gut.

"And you would do anything to protect yours," Rory said with a near-knockout punch.

Jimmy's gaze was unfocused but he recovered quickly. He angled his head toward Rory's shoulder and bared his teeth like he was about to bite. Rory kicked the man away, which gave Jimmy a chance to hop to his feet.

Just as he was about to fire off a blow to the face, Rory was able to roll out of the way and then catch Jimmy's foot. The sound of a bullet splitting the air shocked Rory. He immediately let go of Jimmy and checked himself for blood or signs of an entry point.

Time slowed almost to a stop as his gaze shifted to Emerson, who'd stood up and garnered Theo's weapon. She appeared shocked but in control. Her hands trembled as the back door of the shop slammed open.

"Drop your weapon," an authoritative voice commanded.

Much to Rory's relief, Emerson held the gun out in front of her so the agent could watch her actions. She slowly lowered it to the ground.

"Hands where I can see 'em," the agent continued. He had on a dark blue vest with three letters: FBI.

Jimmy was the only one who didn't raise his hands. He took a step back. The car behind him stopped him from falling as he slid down, a look of shock on his face. It had been enough to stop him cold but Emerson's aim was off if she'd been trying for his heart. Instead, she clipped his right shoulder.

"There's a deputy inside the trash bin," Rory stated. He physically ached to get to Emerson, but he knew better than to aggravate agents with guns, especially when the barrels were pointed in his direction. "The man who has been shot is Jimmy Zenon. I believe he's the person you're looking for."

The next few seconds were filled with agents storming them as emergency vehicles arrived. Theo was lifted out of the bin and laid onto his back. Another agent was busy handcuffing Jimmy. Rory figured he was next along with Emerson. They would be treated as suspects until they could be cleared. Theo was in no condition to stand up for them or explain what had happened.

A woman in dark clothes, sunglasses and a wide-brimmed hat was escorted out the back of the building, heading straight toward them. Wide-brim had a similar build to Emerson's. The lady picked up speed as she focused on Emerson. She dropped down in front of her. The glasses came off first. The hat second. There was enough of a resemblance to know this was Emerson's mother.

"Baby?" she said as tears started rolling down her cheeks and she studied Emerson's eyes. "You're so grown."

"That's what happens when you leave for almost three decades," Emerson stated but there was very little anger in her voice. Shock. Disbelief. Maybe a little hurt.

"I'm so sorry," her mother said as she brought the backs of her fingers up to touch Emerson's cheeks. "Are you really here right now? I feared this day would never come and that I would have to hide like a criminal forever."

"Why did you?" Emerson asked. "If you had evidence against my father and Jimmy's dad? What made you disappear with it?"

"Insurance," she said. "It was simple. As long as I had this, no one ever laid a hand on you."

"You did it for me?" Emerson asked.

"Your father would never allow me to leave. Forget about taking you with me," she said. "He told me once that he had people who would hunt me down if I ever so much as hinted to the authorities about his numerous crimes. If I took you, he said he would kill you and make me watch. I couldn't stay. Not with the beatings. But he never laid a hand on you. In his own way, he loved you."

Naomi studied her daughter.

"Is it too late to start again?" she asked as more of those tears trickled down her face.

"It's never too late for second chances," Emerson said before wrapping her arms around her mother's neck.

STATEMENTS WERE GIVEN. Hugs were doled out. Tears were shed. The last two occurred at Polly's and involved free dessert and coffee.

"How's Theo?" Emerson asked Rory as he sat beside her and listened to her and her mother get acquainted.

"He's roughed up but going to be fine," Rory said. "The hospital is keeping him overnight for observation, but the nurse said he will be released tomorrow. His wife is spending the night while her mother takes care of the kids."

"What a relief," Emerson said, exhaling the breath she'd been holding as Rory read the text from Theo's wife.

"How long have you two been together?" her mother asked as she reached for her handbag.

"Us?" Emerson asked, caught off guard by the question. "We're not—"

"Not long," Rory interrupted, "but enough time to know that I'm in love with your daughter."

"What did you just say?" Emerson asked, unsure if she'd just heard him right. "Because I thought you just said that you're in love with me."

"I am," he confirmed. "I've fallen for you hook, line and sinker."

Normally the words *I love you* caused her to need air. She would be glancing around for her running shoes, but they sounded so right rolling off Rory's tongue that she wanted to plant her feet and stay put.

"I hope you're serious, Rory Hayes, because I'm in love with you too," she said.

Her mother's smile was ear to ear. "I'll leave you two lovebirds alone. I've got to get a good night's sleep tonight so we can spend the day tomorrow catching up."

"You're staying in town?" Emerson asked, hopeful.

"Kid, I'm never leaving you again," her mother said with a laugh. "You'll have to pry me from your side with a crowbar."

"Why don't you stay at the ranch?" Rory asked.

"I wouldn't want to put anyone out," her mother said.

"It's the best way to have coffee with your daughter without anyone having to get in a vehicle and drive," he pointed out. "All I have to do is make one phone call and it'll be set."

"If you're sure it's no trouble," her mother said.

"None at all." He held out his hand. "I can enter the address in your GPS."

Her mother handed over her cell. She leaned toward Emerson's ear and in a church-quiet voice said, "I hope you know how special this one is. I can see how much you love each other. Hang on tight to the good ones."

"I intend to, Mom," she said with a smile.

Rory turned and handed the cell back. He fired off a text from his and then said, "All good. You can follow us but the address is in your phone just in case."

"Well, thank you," her mother said. She turned and winked at Emerson, then gave a slight nod. Emerson knew exactly what her mother was trying to say. "I'll see you there."

Rory offered his hand to Emerson to help her up. She took it and stood.

"You should know that I plan to marry you," she said to him before looping her arms around his neck.

"Well, that's a good thing because I plan to ask," he said before dropping his lips onto hers, where they fit perfectly.

Cheers erupted.

"Before we make this official, I need to ask Liv if it's okay if I marry her father," Emerson said.

"Wouldn't have it any other way," he quipped before lifting her off the floor in an embrace. "And you should know this is for keeps."

"Good," she said, her heart full. "Because that's the only way I play."

Rory's smile was the perfect mix of sexy and sweet. On second thought, a little more on the sexy side. Her sexy Rory. Her home.

Emerson couldn't believe how good life could be, but she was ready to find out.

* * * * *

Look for a new title in USA TODAY
bestselling author Barb Han's
The Cowboys of Cider Creek miniseries when
Trapped in Texas *goes on sale next month!*

And don't miss the first book in the series,
Rescued by the Rancher, *available now wherever*
Harlequin Intrigue books are sold!

COMING NEXT MONTH FROM

H HARLEQUIN

INTRIGUE

#2145 HER BRAND OF JUSTICE
A Colt Brothers Investigation • by B.J. Daniels
Ansley Brookshire's quest to uncover the truth about her adoption leads her to Lonesome, Montana—and into the arms cowboy Buck Crawford. But someone doesn't want the truth to come out...and will do *anything* to halt Ansley and Buck's search. Even kill.

#2146 TRAPPED IN TEXAS
The Cowboys of Cider Creek • by Barb Han
With a deadly stalker closing in, rising country star Raelynn Simmons needs to stay off the stage—and off the grid. Agent Sean Hayes accepts one last mission to keep her safe from danger. But with flying bullets putting them in close proximity, who will keep Sean's heart safe from Raelynn?

#2147 DEAD AGAIN
Defenders of Battle Mountain • by Nichole Severn
Macie Barclay never stopped searching for her best friend's murderer...until a dead body and a new lead reunites her with her ex, Detective Riggs Karig. Riggs knows he and Macie are playing with fire. Especially when she becomes the killer's next target...

#2148 WYOMING MOUNTAIN MURDER
Cowboy State Lawmen • by Juno Rushdan
Charlie Sharp knows how to defend herself. But when a client goes missing—presumed dead—she must rely on Detective Brian Bradshaw to uncover the truth. As they dig for clues and discover more dead bodies, all linked to police corruption, can they learn to trust each other to survive?

#2149 OZARKS DOUBLE HOMICIDE
Arkansas Special Agents • by Maggie Wells
A grisly double homicide threatens Michelle Fraser's yearslong undercover assignment. But the biggest threat to the FBI agent is Lieutenant Ethan Scott. He knows the seemingly innocent attorney is hiding something. But when they untangle a political money laundering conspiracy, how far will he go to keep Michelle's secrets?

#2150 DANGER IN THE NEVADA DESERT
by Denise N. Wheatley
Nevada's numeric serial killer is on a rampage—and his crimes are getting personal. When Sergeant Charlotte Bowman teams up with Detective Miles Love to capture the deranged murderer before another life is lost, they must fight grueling, deadly circumstances...and their undeniable attraction.

**YOU CAN FIND MORE INFORMATION ON UPCOMING HARLEQUIN TITLES,
FREE EXCERPTS AND MORE AT HARLEQUIN.COM.**

HICNM0423

HARLEQUIN
PLUS

Try the best multimedia subscription service for romance readers like you!

Read, Watch and Play.

Experience the easiest way to get the romance content you crave.

Start your **FREE TRIAL** at
www.harlequinplus.com/freetrial.